K=2

24

Biscuit-Shooter

Center Point
Large Print

**This Large Print Book carries the
Seal of Approval of N.A.V.H.**

Biscuit-Shooter

CLIFTON ADAMS

CENTER POINT LARGE PRINT
THORNDIKE, MAINE

This Center Point Large Print edition
is published in the year 2015 by arrangement with
Golden West Literary Agency.

Copyright © 1971 by Clifton Adams.

The text of this Large Print edition is unabridged.
In other aspects, this book may vary
from the original edition.
Printed in the United States of America
on permanent paper.
Set in 16-point Times New Roman type.

ISBN: 978-1-62899-631-9 (hardcover)
ISBN: 978-1-62899-636-4 (paperback)

Library of Congress Cataloging-in-Publication Data

Adams, Clifton.
Biscuit-shooter / Clifton Adams. — Center Point Large Print edition.
pages cm
Summary: "When Willie McGuire accidentally breaks Jeremy Hooker's
leg, the gunfighter offers a $1000 reward for Willie's capture. What
follows is a tale of pursuit and escape, spiced with the humorous antics
of a well-intentioned but bungling cowboy"—Provided by publisher.
ISBN 978-1-62899-631-9 (hardcover : alk. paper)
ISBN 978-1-62899-636-4 (pbk. : alk. paper)
1. Large type books. I. Title.
PS3551.D34B57 2015
813'.54—dc23

2015016885

one

It was true that some folks did not take right off to Willie McGuire. Even his sidekick, Pinto Gonzales, had to admit that riding with McGuire was often an aggravating experience—not to mention exasperating, annoying, irksome, and risky. However, life had been relatively peaceful for the last month. Rarely did Willie ride more than a day out of his way to look for a fight— Pinto innocently took this as evidence that his pard was mending his ways.

That, at least, had been his impression until about seven hours ago.

Sometime during the night they had made camp on the bank of some nameless gyp creek near the main cattle trail to Dodge. Now the first flinty light of dawn lay on the prairie, and McGuire was sitting on his blanket, cautiously examining a large lump behind his left ear.

For some time Willie McGuire had been tracking down an assortment of bruises, bites, scratches, cuts, and lumps that seemed to cover his hulking frame from one distant extreme to the other. Pinto eyed him with a look of expectation but said nothing. He busied himself with the fire, reboiling some old Arbuckle's grounds left over from several camps ago.

McGuire paused for a moment in his examination and peered blearily out at the monotonous prairie. "Wonder whereabouts we're at," he asked at last.

"Somewheres between the Canadian and the Palo Duro," Pinto told him. "Near as I can figger."

Despite his easygoing nature, there were certain peculiarities in the character of Willie McGuire that an impartial observer could not ignore. For one thing, he tended to change jobs more often than other cowhands. These changes usually followed a violent exchange of opinions with some ranch strawboss. Also, he had an extraordinary fondness for white corn whiskey. And contrariness and stubbornness were the most conspicuous aspects of his character.

There had been a time, Pinto remembered, when Willie had been known by the name of "Jackass" McGuire. Willie had assumed it was because of the long-eared animal that he was riding at the time, but Pinto had known better. No matter. Willie had borne the name with pride. Even now he greatly admired the jackass for its princely air of independence, its strength, its total deafness to any sound resembling an order. He delighted in the animal's ability to twist its neck at impossible angles in order to bite the leg of any man fool enough to try to ride it, not to mention that beast's penchant for kicking all locked gates and doors to smithereens.

"Pumas," as McGuire liked to point out, "ain't nothin' but overgrowed tomcats. One time in a tent show up at Caldwell I seen pumas jumpin' through burnin' barrel hoops. And grizzly bears, why I seen bears dance the do-si-do a sight sprier than most cowhands I know. But let me ask you how many jackasses you ever seen jiggin' the fandango or jumpin' through barrel hoops! I can tell you," he would conclude confidentially. "Nobody yet has ever seen a trained jackass. You can work till you're blue in the face but you won't never learn a jackass a thing. And why is that? Boys, I'll tell you. Ever'thin' that's worth learnin', a jackass already knows it by heart!"

Unfortunately, there had been a greenhorn in Abilene with the poor sense to laugh at Willie's adopted name. The short burst of laughter had been followed by several broken bones and a great deal of shattered furniture. Several weeks later, when the town marshal turned Willie out of jail, Pinto had persuaded him to take up his own name again.

That was the way it was when you parded with a man like Willie. Life, as long as it lasted, was usually interesting.

At the moment McGuire held his head in his hands and groaned. "Whereabouts," he asked haltingly, "was we at last night?"

"You don't recollect?"

Willie shook his head and winced. "What I got

7

to do is leave off drinkin' that rotgut whiskey in them trail town saloons."

"That ought to be easy," Pinto said dryly. "Seein' that we ain't got a single two-bit piece between us."

Cautiously, McGuire felt in his pockets. They were empty. "What happened?"

"The town marshal rifled our pockets to pay for the furniture you busted."

It was beginning to come to McGuire in disconnected flashes. Trail town saloon. Laughter. Argument. Brawl. "That marshal never had no right to rifle our pockets."

"He figgered we never had no right to bust up the saloon."

"The wheel of fortune was rigged."

If it hadn't been the wheel of fortune it would have been the faro layout. Or shaved dice. Or watered whiskey. That's the way things happened when you rode with McGuire.

"Well," McGuire groaned philosophically, "it ain't nothin' to stew over. We'll be raisin' the Bar-A herd sometime today. That ramrod said we could hire on as drovers rest of the way to Dodge."

"That ramrod was missin' a set of front teeth the last I seen of him. It was the Bar-A bunch that you tangled with."

Willie McGuire stared blearily at the mahogany face of his pal. "Maybe," he said weakly, "I'll take some of that coffee."

McGuire took some of the scalding coffee, burning his mouth on the lip of the tin cup. Gradually he began to notice that Pinto was watching him with an air of quiet expectancy.

With growing uneasiness, Willie told him, "You're startin' to look like the first hog at the sloppin' trough. Is there somethin' you ain't told me?"

"How much do you recollect about last night?"

"Well . . ." McGuire scratched himself thoughtfully. "There was a to-do about the wheel of fortune. Then the fandango."

"The poker table?" Pinto prodded.

McGuire stared blankly.

"You fell across the table."

McGuire looked dazed and uninterested.

"Scattered checks and players from Hell to Houston," Pinto continued in a casual tone. A bit *too* casual, if Willie had paused to reflect on it.

"I don't recollect."

"Cat-eyed dude with a shammy-skin vest and pocket holsters."

McGuire dimly recalled the eyes and the vest. "What about him?"

"That was Jeremy Hooker."

McGuire's bloodshot eyes opened wide. "Well, well . . ." He was impressed. With Wes Hardin in prison and Will Bonnie dead, and John Ringo and most of the other big gunslingers dead or behind bars, Jeremy Hooker had the killing business just about to himself. "What do you know about that?" Willie said in wonder. "Runnin' into Jeremy Hooker in a place like . . ."

"Tar City." Pinto was feeding it to him slowly.

"How come a killer like Hooker to be in a place like that?"

"Can't say about that. But I expect he'll be stayin' on for a spell."

"How come?" McGuire asked, his interest waning.

"Because last night you busted his leg."

In a violent fit of coughing, McGuire spewed coffee all the way across the fire. Suddenly, and with frightening clarity, he recalled the misunderstanding with the dude. "How you know his leg's busted?"

"From the way he was hollerin' and the funny way it was twisted under him when you let him go."

McGuire rubbed a nervous hand across his mouth. A good barroom tussle, he'd always claimed, was good for a man. But tangling with gunslingers was not his line. "How long," he asked uneasily, "do you figger it takes a leg to mend?"

Pinto shrugged. "Depends on whose leg and who sets it."

"Three, four weeks?"

"Maybe."

Willie McGuire took a long, deep breath and shook the fog from his brain. "I just made up my mind," he said with conviction. "It's time we rolled our beds and traveled. But not," he added reasonably, "on an empty belly."

Pinto attended to the rolls and saddled the horses while McGuire shakily fried dry-salt meat and panbread. McGuire, who ordinarily took considerable pride in his abilities as a cook, this morning spilled grease in the fire and upset the coffee while casting frequent glances over his shoulder in the direction of Tar City.

The two men hunkered down next to the fire and divided the meat and bread between them, and McGuire began boiling another batch of coffee in the greasy skillet. For several minutes they ate in silence. Finally McGuire scratched the blue-black stubble on his jutting chin and asked worriedly, "You figger Hooker's goin' to be sore about that leg of his?"

Gonzales looked at him and grinned.

". . . I guess he will," McGuire sighed. They wolfed their breakfast, finished the coffee, and settled back for a few moments to build their first smokes of the day. McGuire thoughtfully studied his hands as he lit his brownpaper cigarette— they weren't exactly shaking, but he had seen them steadier. Pinto—lean, brown, hawkish— watched him with the inscrutibility of a Chinese gandy dancer.

"We'd be toler'bly safe," McGuire dreamed, "if we could just hook up with that Bar-A outfit."

"Put it out of your head," Pinto advised him.

"Bad as that, huh?"

"Busted teeth was just part of that ramrod's damage, and maybe not the worst part at that."

Willie McGuire sighed with resignation. "Which way you figger we ought to head?"

Pinto considered for a moment. "South. If worst comes to worst, I've got pals in Chihuahua."

McGuire shrugged his massive shoulders. A tragic figure, cruelly used by the caprice of Fate.

They traveled south, carefully skirting the canyon of the Palo Duro which was too thickly settled by cowmen for McGuire's liking. He wasn't really worried—he kept telling himself—that Jeremy Hooker would come looking for him. By the time the gunman's leg mended and he was fit to ride again, most likely he'd have better things to do than to come gunning for a nobody named Willie McGuire.

Nevertheless, McGuire reasoned, with Pinto heartily concurring, it never hurt to be a little careful. So for three days they scrupulously avoided settlements and line camps and even the sod huts of squatter farmers. At the end of that time they found themselves on the banks of a freshwater stream that Pinto remembered as White Fish Creek. They continued on to the Old Mobeetie Road and the south fork of the Red. Over to the west, according to a treaty of 1865,

12

was the Comanche hunting grounds. But the Indians hadn't been near it for almost a dozen years. It was cow country now. The Comanches were on their reservation in Indian Territory.

McGuire gazed out at the wasteland and heaved a sigh of relief. "Tell you the truth," he said to his partner, "I've got about all the saddle galls I can use. How about lightin' here by the water and makin' camp?"

Pinto shrugged. "We're out of grub and coffee."

"We can shoot some grub."

"All right. But we'd still be out of coffee."

That was the trouble with Gonzales. Every time McGuire had a notion that was comfortable and pleasurable, Pinto thought up a hatful of reasons why they couldn't do it. Nevertheless, it was a fact that a plainsman like Willie McGuire would almost as soon lose his saddle as his last handful of Arbuckle's coffee.

Once again they reined to the south, with the July sun burning over the hulking gray bluffs of Cap Rock far to their right. Once, McGuire mused to himself, this had been the Comanche war trail to Mexico. Might be they'd stay with it all the way to Chihuahua. Not that he was actually *afraid* of that gunslinger, but what with stampedes and cut banks and electrical storms, the life of a cowhand was dangerous enough as it stood. No sense making it more so by aggravating a killer like Hooker.

Pinto rose slightly in his saddle and pointed a long brown finger straight ahead. "What do you make of that?"

Willie looked at the low-lying reddish cloud far to the south. It hugged the distant horizon like a ground fog and was moving slowly toward the northwest. "Trail herd," McGuire grunted. "Big one, from the looks of that dust."

Pinto shot a look at his partner. Both men were getting the same idea. "You figger maybe they're lookin' to hire on a couple of trail hands?" Willie asked hopefully.

"Wouldn't do any damage to find out." There was a wistful note in Pinto's words. Tying up with a big trail outfit would be the best insurance they could have against a killer like Hooker. Once you signed on with a big herd, you were a part of a family. And the family looked out for its own, even against gunslingers. Chances were they could stick with the herd all the way to Dodge, and Hooker would never be the wiser.

If there were any openings for extra riders. And *if* McGuire's unpredictable temper didn't get them thrown out of the cow camp before the subject of work could be brought up.

Willie gazed at the approaching cloud with a happy grin. Strong coffee and hot grub was what the herd meant to him. Sourdough biscuits and fried steak, with flour gravy on the side. Arbuckle's coffee strong enough to float horseshoes. He rose in the stirrups and squinted out at the brown prairie. "If we can find the wagon, we ought to make it just in time for supper."

"That," Pinto said dryly, "ought to make Cookie happy."

Pinto Gonzales watched the distant herd with an experienced eye. A thousand head, he judged, and maybe more. There would be twelve to fourteen hands working a herd that size. At least a dozen ravenous appetites for the wagon cook to satisfy three times a day prepared from a kitchen that was always on the move, in a country where the water was gypy and fuel scarce. It was not surprising that most wagon cooks were as touchy as she-wolfs with pups. Still, for a trail boss to turn away a hungry guest was unthinkable. The cook was obliged to feed any hand that appeared in the grub line, a frontier custom that Willie and Pinto had taken advantage of more than once.

For an hour they rode in the direction of the slowly moving cloud. The sun was slanting sharply to the west, and Willie McGuire's long face was taking on a worried look. Within another hour supper would be over. Latecomers would have to take the leavings—and Willie knew from experience that there were precious few leavings at a chuck wagon.

After another several minutes one of the outfit's swing riders appeared hazing a stray out of a gully. Willie stood in the stirrups and hollered, "Which way to the wagon?"

The dusty cowhand reined up for a moment and pointed generally to the southwest. He was grinning widely. Even at a distance of almost three hundred yards, Pinto could see the grin, and there was something about it that struck a jangling note in his mind.

They rode for another half hour before raising the wagon. Topping a rise, they looked down on the welcome sight, sniffed the heady aroma of burning sage and frying steaks. Far in the distance, almost a mile away, was the main bed-ground where the cattle were slowly milling. Maybe half a mile downwind from the wagon, the night wrangler was getting set to take over the remuda.

"Can you see what outfit it is?" Willie asked, his stomach growling with anticipation.

Pinto shook his head. "The brand's on the wagon, but it's too far away to make it out."

"You don't reckon that Bar-A herd would be this far south, do you?"

Pinto smiled faintly. "For the good of my stomach, I hope not."

They nudged their horses forward, careful to approach the wagon on the leeward so that their dust wouldn't settle on the cook's evening efforts. Willie counted six hands hunkered down in the brush, forming a rough half circle in front of the wagon, eating their last meal of the day. That, he guessed, would be half of the crew; the other half would be getting the cattle bedded down for the night.

"Circle-M," Pinto said when they got closer, reading the brand burned on the side of the wagon. He was not familiar with the brand; but then there were a lot of cattle outfits in Texas, no cowhand could be expected to know them all. They staked their horses well away from the wagon and came forward on foot.

"Howdy," Willie McGuire said, happily eying the tall stack of cooked steaks on the chuck wagon's letdown table.

"Howdy." A big fairhaired giant of a man dumped his tin plate and cup into the wreck pan beneath the wagon. "If you boys are lookin' for grub, dig in and help yourselves." He flashed a wide, toothy grin back at some of the other hands. They grinned back at him. It suddenly seemed to Pinto that the dusk was filled with those wide, secret grins.

The cook came around the side of the wagon and looked them over sullenly—which was perfectly normal for a wagon cook.

"You notice anything queer here?" Pinto asked his partner from the side of his mouth.

Willie, with eyes only for the cook's biscuit ovens and fried steaks, had accepted the grins as a show of pleasure, on the part of the hands, for the

17

honor of having a McGuire eat with them. Pinto sighed to himself. He had a sinking feeling that the mystery of the grins would soon be revealed.

Following the custom of the country, the two men splashed themselves with water at the wash-stand on the far side of the wagon, letting it be known that they were not greenhorns or tramps but experienced cowhands who knew their way around in a chuck line. Willie rubbed his hands together and said to the unsmiling cook, "That coffee smells strong enough to load a gun with! Whereabouts are the eatin' irons?"

The cook, a rangy, rawboned man in his middle years, crossed his arms across his dirty apron and pointed in his sullen way, with his chin. Willie dipped into the equipment box and found his tin plate and cup and other tools. It seemed to Pinto that the grins had frozen on the faces of the other diners. Expectant grins. Almost fearful grins. Suddenly Pinto had a feeling that he had experienced many times since he first hooked up with Willie McGuire. In the pit of his stomach there was the cold assurance that a grave—maybe fatal—mistake had been made, and he would very shortly learn just what that mistake had been.

McGuire, experiencing none of his pal's anxiety, stepped boldly up and stabbed a piece of steak with his fork. Immediately a look of disappointment—and then outright disapproval—showed in his long, unhandsome face. Scowling, he held the piece of meat up to the light of the early evening sky and inspected it closely. He brought it closer to his eye and studied it some more. By this time the expression on his face was unmistakable disgust. "Hell's fire," he announced to the prairie at large, "I've seen cows get well that was hurt worse than the one this steak came off of!"

Pinto winced and braced himself for violence as Willie replaced the slightly undone piece of meat and rummaged in the pile of steaks until he found one that was cooked enough to suit him. The dining cowhands seemed to be holding their breaths. There was a curious, strained expression in their faces. Their eyes bulged. Their expectant looks went from Willie to the cook and back to Willie again.

McGuire oblivious to all this attention, helped himself to coffee and gravy and sourdough biscuits, while the cook slowly unfolded his arms, picked up a heavy pothook and regarded it with affection.

"Listen," Pinto said earnestly, after he had filled his own plate, "makin' an enemy out of the cook ain't no way to get hired on as a trail hand."

"You couldn't hardly call him a *cook*," McGuire said complacently. "Anybody that would serve raw meat to workin' cowhands and call it steak."

It was useless to explain to McGuire that some men might not *like* their steak burned to a cinderlike doneness, and Pinto Gonzales didn't try. The two men hunkered down together close to the coffee fire, crossed their legs with the precision of music hall dancers and balanced their plates on their ankles. "Keep in mind that there's a killer on our trail," Pinto said quietly while gazing innocently at the far horizon. "Or soon will be. As soon as he mends. Hookin' up with an outfit like this one might be the only way of gettin' out of the country alive."

McGuire nodded absently. "After supper we'll talk to the wagon boss." He cut off a piece of meat and began chewing. "Tough," he said thoughtfully, as though a dependent world had been waiting for his pronouncement. "Ought to of been pounded more before cookin'."

The big cook glared at them from the wagon tailgate and hefted an iron skillet in his hand. "What he done wrong," McGuire said with the profound authority of an expert, "was put the salt on the meat before puttin' it in the fat. Any fool ought to know better'n . . ."

Pinto jabbed him with an elbow. "It's a hot meal, and it's free. And if there's any openings on the crew, we could use the work."

Pinto had the disquieting feeling that all eyes in camp were boring into the back of his head. The cook sidled away from the fire and moved into the shadows. Pinto noticed that he was still holding onto the heavy skillet.

McGuire popped a sourdough biscuit into his

mouth, clamped his jaws on it and began chewing. After several minutes of concentrated chewing and swallowing, he exploded indignantly. "Gawd-amighty, boys, I've seen men shot dead with bullets that was softer'n these sourdoughs!"

That was when Pinto heard the sound behind them. It was the cook making an angry, growling sound in his throat. Almost at the same instant the skillet struck Willie McGuire's head.

McGuire made a small sound, a little grunt of surprise, before pitching forward in a dead heap. His last expression was one of disbelief that anyone would so cruelly attack a harmless, well-intentioned, likable cowhand like himself.

two

Tar City had not been the same since the fracas between the Bar-A drovers and the big cowhand named McGuire. Some citizens doubted it would ever be the same again. Visiting trail hands—the few who came to Tar City out of necessity—tramped the plankwalks quietly. There was little drinking and no horseplay in the town that was noted for its rowdiness.

The presence of Jeremy Hooker saw to that. Jeremy Hooker, with his temper rubbed raw with fever and pain—and the frustration of not being able—thus far, at least—to kill the man who had broken his leg.

Doc Wilford Mulley, Tar City's druggist and part-time physician and veterinarian, stood in front of the livery barn watching Hooker's window with a cautious eye. For the best part of four days the gunslinger had been sitting there at his second-story window, gazing balefully down at the town and the prairie. He rarely spoke, except in icy threats. He just sat there, his injured leg propped on a chair, his deadly little double-action .38 in his lap or in his hand, angrily waiting for the moment when he could shuck his plaster of paris cast and find and kill the man called Willie McGuire.

Doc Mulley sighed and mopped his forehead with a blue bandanna. Hooker was the first professional killer he had ever tended, and he hoped he would be the last. The doc glanced ruefully at his faintly trembling hands. He was not a drinking man, except in a sociable way, but this morning he had stopped at the saloon for a steadying drink before making his daily visit to the killer's room. It was those eyes, Doc decided, that were so hard on the nerves. Those snakelike eyes that bored into you and silently sized you up, as if they were measuring you for a coffin.

Mulley was of half a notion to pay another quick visit to the Drover Saloon. But at that moment Hooker, as if he had been reading the doc's mind, leaned out of the window and called in his cold, emotionless voice, "Get yourself up here, Mulley!"

Resignedly, Mulley mounted the outside stairs of the Tar City Hotel. Hooker's boxboard room was bake-oven hot, when the doc entered it, but the killer's curiously yellow face was as dry as stone.

While the doc went through the motions of inspecting the leg, Hooker gazed bleakly out at the prairie. There was nothing more that Mulley could do about the broken bone, and the gunman knew it, but it seemed to amuse him to have the doc on hand, jumping at his whims. "Not much life in town," he said dryly. "You reckon that might be on account of Jeremy Hooker's settin' here one day after the other, runnin' over with bile?"

Doc Mulley cleared his throat but could think of nothing to say. Hooker laughed suddenly, a dry, rustling sound. "It's goin' to get worse, Doc. This here'll be a ghost town in a little while if this leg don't mend so I can ride out of here."

"I'm doin' all I can, Mr. Hooker. It's goin' to take time."

"Time is somethin' I ain't got a lot of. Time and patience. Has Hargarty got back yet?"

Frank Hargarty was the town marshal and, for the present, the only lawman in the county. Directly after Hooker's misfortune in the saloon brawl, the county sheriff sized up the situation and decided to go on a wolf hunt with some local cowmen. "I think I seen the marshal's horse at the livery corral," Mulley said, closing his satchel. "I'll tell him you want to see him."

"You do that," the gunman said grimly.

It was midmorning when Marshal Hargarty, just back from two days of questioning ranchers and travelers, entered the killer's room. He was a stocky, slow-moving ex-cowhand, good enough at his job when it came to handling crooked cardsharks and drunken drovers. But he was no gunslinger. Neither was he a fool. His only plans concerning Jeremy Hooker were to get along with

25

him, not start any trouble, and get him out of Tar City as soon as possible.

The gunman spoke to Hargarty without bothering to look away from the window. "Did you find McGuire?"

"I talked to more'n a dozen ranchers, and I don't know how many travelers, and none of them has seen McGuire. I got draymen and wagoners and stage drivers watchin' all the main roads through the county. Sooner or later McGuire and his sidekick—a Mex by the name of Gonzales—will have to leave the ridges. When they take to a road or land in a settlement, I'll hear about it."

"What," Hooker asked coldly, still gazing out at the prairie, "if they decide to hook up with a cattle outfit comin' up the trail?"

"That," the marshal confessed with some discomfort, "will be a different proposition. Drovers like to hang together. They could cause trouble, even wreck the town, if a town marshal tried to arrest one of their hands."

For the first time Hooker turned from the window and looked at the local marshal. "I don't care about the town, Hargarty. And I don't care about you. If McGuire slips through my fingers because of you . . ." He raised his .38 and idly glanced along the barrel in the marshal's direction.

With the gunman's threat ringing in his ears, the lawman began to sweat. He licked his dry lips and looked pained in the effort of concentration. "I know some old-time drovers, most of them with supply outfits along the trail. I'll get them to look out for McGuire and let me know if he's in any of the outfits comin' this way."

Hooker closed his steely eyes for a moment, turning the lawman's proposition in his mind. Slowly, he began to smile. He liked the plan. With wagoners and stage drivers and mail carriers watching the main roads, the cattle trail was the only door left open to McGuire. And that door was about to be closed.

"Of course," the marshal said nervously, "locatin' McGuire is one thing, gettin' him away from his outfit will be somethin' else."

But Hooker was not worried about that. He had his own plan for taking care of McGuire, as soon as he found out where he was. "You just find him," he said in a tone that was almost genial. "You find him, Marshal. And leave the rest to me."

That night, as the Tar City marshal was getting word to his friends in drover supply houses along the Western Trail, Pinto Gonzales was bending over his unconscious pal with a look of mild concern on his brown face. The big fairhaired drover, who turned out to be the trail boss and whose name was Arnie Stone, opened McGuire's glassy eyes with his fingers and said, "He looks dead to me."

But Pinto had seen Willie in this condition before. He rolled his sidekick over on his back and shook him vigorously. "Has anybody got any whiskey?"

"I don't allow whiskey on a cattle drive," Arnie Stone told him.

Pinto shrugged. "Lemon extract will do. Or vanilla, or whatever you've got."

Grudgingly, Stone had one of the men go through the cook's store of flavorings and see what he could find. He came back after a while with a pint bottle half full of yellowish liquid. Pinto sniffed it to assure himself that it was lemon, Willie's favorite flavor. He unlocked McGuire's jaws and dribbled some into his mouth.

Willie McGuire began to sputter and cough. His eyes fluttered open. He pawed the air wildly, like a possum falling from a high limb. Pinto gave him some more of the extract. The Circle-M drovers crowded around, their mouths open, marveling at the resurrection. The cook, with the lethal skillet still in his hand, was the most surprised of all. "I hit him hard enough," he complained, "to kill a bull!" He sounded bitterly disappointed at Willie's unexpected return to life.

For several seconds McGuire went on sputtering and cursing and gulping from the bottle. Then Stone wrestled the bottle from him and corked it before it was quite empty. "Mister," he said heavily, "you better lay still for a spell. Cookie here just dented his skillet on the back of your head."

With extreme caution, McGuire shoved himself to a sitting position and felt of the egg-sized lump behind his left ear. It was coming back to him now. The sullen cook. The tough sourdoughs. The iron skillet flying out of the night like a thunderbolt.

Pinto Gonzales said in a tone of utmost reasonableness, "McGuire, don't do it."

McGuire looked at him and grinned wolfishly. "I ain't goin' to do nothin', except maybe kill me a dough-puncher." With enormous determination, McGuire got himself to his feet, rising hind end first, like a cow pulling itself out of a bog. The cook looked on with amazed blankness. The other drovers began to shake off their own stunned disbelief. Expectant grins appeared as the cook began backing worriedly away. Obviously the cook was not the most popular member of the outfit, and some of the hands were eager to see his surliness rewarded.

The cook shot a nervous glance at the trail boss. "Get him out of camp, Stone! Before I shut his big mouth permanent!" He brandished the skillet in one hand, the pothook in the other. But he was like an old range bull that bellows and paws the dirt instead of rushing into the fight. More show than guts.

Arnie Stone sized the situation up quickly, then

folded his arms across his chest and said mildly, "You dealt yourself in, Cookie. You oughtn't to of hit him with that skillet if you wasn't lookin' for a fight."

One of the drovers laughed. Another one called, with a certain amount of glee, "Back off, boys, and give them room!" Almost at the same instant McGuire let out a roar and threw himself at the cook. But the cook was more agile than Willie had expected; he easily side-stepped the bull-like rush and clouted his tormentor with the pothook. Then, with neat precision, he whirled and hit Willie again with the skillet as he was going down. That was the last thing McGuire remembered for some time.

After considerable pain and long darkness, McGuire forced himself to open one eye. Pinto was hunkered down beside him, idly smoking a cigarette. One shift had returned to the herd at bedground and another had come to the wagon for supper. The cowhands were sitting around the fire trench, methodically chewing their steak and biscuits, quietly watching to see what the big stranger would do this time when he returned to life.

Slowly, McGuire brought the scene into focus. He rolled over onto one side, wincing at the pain in his head. The cook was nowhere to be seen. Neither was Arnie Stone. From his bed of pain, McGuire looked up at his partner and croaked, "Is there any more of that lemon extract?"

"The trail boss says he already let you have all he can spare."

McGuire cursed the trail boss for his meanness, but with no great enthusiasm. One of the cowhands filled a tin cup with coffee and handed it to Willie with a grin. "Cookie was a mean one," he said good-naturedly. "Don't feel bad. You ain't the first one to come out second best in a tussle with that one."

Willie tasted the coffee and made a face. "His coffee ain't no better'n his sourdoughs." But before he said it he looked around to make sure that the cook was not listening. Willie McGuire was bullheaded and stubborn, but he was slowly learning to respect the cook's ability to fight with a skillet, if not to cook with it. Painfully, he shoved himself to a sitting position and squinted into the night. "Where's he at now?"

Pinto dropped his cigarette into the fire trench. "The cook drawed his time and rode. Said he wouldn't stay hooked up with an outfit that wouldn't stand up for him in a fight."

Willie felt gingerly of his battered head. "The outfit's better off without him," he said sourly. "His cookin' wasn't fit to eat, anyhow."

"But better'n no cookin' at all," Pinto pointed out dryly. He built and lit another cigarette and said in a tone that was elaborately casual, "The trail boss says we can sign on with the outfit the rest of the way to Dodge."

31

McGuire stopped rubbing his head and put the hostile wagon cook out of his mind. "That's good!" He dreamed for a minute of Dodge City saloons, gambling hall girls, and barrels of red whiskey. "Yes sir, Jeremy Hooker won't never find us stuck away in the middle of this herd."

Pinto smiled, his teeth gleaming wetly in the firelight. "I've already peeled the horses and turned them into the remuda."

Willie nodded. This was a comfortable and thoroughly familiar routine. At one time or another they had worked on a dozen trail drives, and one drive was much the same as any other. The dawn to night hours, plus the hours of night watch. The dust, the storms, the stampedes, the swollen rivers. "What watch do we take tonight?" He was hoping for the last watch, for he felt sorely in need of rest before climbing into the saddle again.

"You can get yourself some sleep," Pinto told him, once again dropping into a tone of extreme casualness. "I'll roust you out when time comes— I'll be nighthawkin'."

Willie made a sound of sympathy. The night wrangler's job, as any drover knew, was the toughest job in the outfit. For several minutes they sat over coffee and smokes. They could hear the sound of cattle, but the herd seemed a long way off. The other drovers had either bedded down or were doing their time at night watch. The

Circle-M wagon stood alone on the prairie, the wagon tongue pointed toward the north star, a lantern hanging from the end of it to show returning drovers the way to their beds.

"Have you started thinkin' about breakfast yet?" Pinto asked after the long silence.

"Breakfast?" McGuire cocked his aching head to one side and considered the sound of the word. It had a pleasant, aromatic ring to it. It evoked the steamy magic of hot coffee on a cold morning, of lightly browned sourdoughs and frying steaks. "What about breakfast?"

Pinto got to his feet. He had learned long ago that it was best to assume a defensive position when confronting McGuire with unpleasant news. "I guess I forgot to mention it. You're the outfit's new biscuit-shooter."

"I ain't no goddamn dough-puncher," Willie McGuire said indignantly.

Pinto assumed an air of surprise. "That ain't the notion you gave the trail boss when you was doin' all that complainin' about the grub. He figgered you was a regular expert."

"Well," Willie confessed with customary modesty, "maybe I am a expert, but that don't mean I aim to spend the rest of this drive over a cookfire." He shoved himself to his feet, his chin jutting stubbornly. "A cowhand has to do a lot of work that he doesn't like. Diggin' postholes, mendin' fence and such. But wranglin' dough and beefsteak is carryin' a thing too far!" Huffily, he jerked his hat down on his battered head and stalked away from the wagon.

"Where you headed?" Pinto asked quietly.

"To catch my dun and ride away from this outfit. Anybody that schemes to catch Willie McGuire and put him in a cook apron is loco!"

During this excited exchange Willie failed to notice the two horsebackers approaching from the direction of the herd. The two riders, one of them Arnie Stone, left their horses some distance from the wagon and started toward the fire as Willie headed toward the remuda.

"McGuire . . ."

There was something in the trail boss's tone that caused Willie to pull up short. "Are you the Willie McGuire," Stone went on, "that had the tussle with Jeremy Hooker a few days ago in Tar City?"

McGuire felt as if someone had touched his back with a knife point. After four days his memory of the gunslinger had begun to pale. He had almost convinced himself that the broken leg was mostly Pinto's imagination. The trail boss walked up to him and looked him in the face. "Are you that Willie McGuire?" he asked again.

Back through the misty memory of that night, Willie could see those snakelike eyes. He cleared his throat with some difficulty. "What if I am?"

"This here's Shorty Eller." Stone indicated the square-set young man beside him. "Shorty's been out scoutin' for water and just got back a little while ago. He come through a place called Warfield, maybe five, six miles over toward the Cap Rock. You want to tell him about it, Shorty?"

The scout looked up into McGuire's face and grinned. Like most short men, he enjoyed seeing a big man squirm. "Looks like you got yourself a pack of trouble, mister. Yes sir, that's just what it looks like to me. Like I was tellin' the boss here . . ."

Stone looked at his scout and seemed to sigh. "Get on with it, Shorty."

Reluctantly, Eller abandoned the fancy work and got to the point. "Well, there's this place called Warfield, where the town marshal's stoppin' ever'body comin' in from Tar City. He looks you over from top to bottom to make sure you ain't the one he's lookin' for, then he starts shootin' questions at you."

"Tell him what kind of questions," the trail boss said.

"Well, first thing he asked about was did I know a big, mean-faced Irishman by the name of McGuire. Or his Mex sidekick, Gonzales. I said I never seen either one of you. And he says let him know if I do—if I knowed what was healthy for me—because Jeremy Hooker was laid up in Tar City with a busted leg and was mighty anxious to know where he could find you. He says that Hooker would be mighty put out if somebody was

35

to know where this McGuire was hidin' and didn't tell him about it. Well . . ." Shorty Eller grinned widely. "There ain't many men that's in any big hurry to make a enemy out of Jeremy Hooker."

"Tell him who you met on your way back to the herd," the trail boss prodded.

"Cookie," the scout said promptly. "Mad as a wet hen. Said he was quittin' the outfit and to hell with it. Said the whole bunch could starve, for all he give a damn."

"Tell him which way Cookie was headed."

"Makin' a beeline right for Warfield. Like as not he's run into that marshal by this time and tellin' him ever'thing he knows. By mornin' I figger Hooker'll have the information he wants."

For once in his life Willie McGuire could think of nothing to say. He could feel beads of sweat on his forehead. His stomach felt as if it had curled up and was hiding behind his liver. He looked helplessly at his sidekick, but Pinto only looked back calmly and said, "You still got it in mind not to take Cookie's job for a spell?"

McGuire gazed up at the dark summer sky, his Adam's apple bobbing convulsively. "You figger that marshal will actually go to Tar City and tell Hooker?"

"That's what I'd do if I was in the marshal's place. I wouldn't want that gunshark mad at *me*."

"We could light out of here," Willie said hopefully, "and make a run for Chihuahua before Hooker's in shape to ride again."

"And run into another marshal in some other town?" the trail boss asked dryly. "Besides that, your horses are played out; you wouldn't make it halfway to Chihuahua."

Willie worried this in his mind and came to a conclusion. "Boys, I aim to ride as far as I can, and then I'll walk." With new determination he turned and headed for the remuda.

Pinto Gonzales looked at Arnie Stone and sighed. "Much obliged for the grub and coffee. Wish we could stay and help with the dishes, but . . ." He shrugged. "This is how it is when you ride with McGuire." With a polite nod, he shouldered his saddle and roll and followed his partner into the darkness.

From the position of the stars Pinto decided that it was about an hour past midnight. They had been riding steadily for five hours. The glow of Cookie's lantern on the end of the wagon tongue had long since dissolved into the night. At last Pinto said, "That trail boss was right about one thing; the horses are tired. They need a rest, and so do we." He pointed toward a distant dark line drawn across the prairie. "Looks like a creek of some kind up ahead. What say we make camp for the rest of the night?"

McGuire agreed that a short rest wouldn't hurt

any of them. He had recovered from his spell of nerves; once again the threat of Jeremy Hooker seemed far in the misty distance. A good week's travel would put them to the Bravo and over the line into Mexico where Pinto's pals would look after them if it came to that. "I ain't worried about this old dun," he said, patting the animal's withers. "Me and him's come a long ways together, and I expect we'll go a heap farther."

It was a few minutes after that utterance that the dun began to favor its off foreleg. Willie got down and inspected the hoof, but there was little that could be done before daylight. A stone bruise, a poorly placed nail in the shoe, a small stone in the frog. Whatever it was it would have to wait for more light. Resignedly, Willie took the reins and led the rest of the way to the creek.

The next morning McGuire inspected the damaged hoof with a sinking heart. It was only a bruise—with a few days' rest the dun would be as good as new. But the pragmatic Gonzales was quick to point out that time was all on the side of Jeremy Hooker. By midmorning they were remembering the security of the trail herd with a certain nostalgia.

At midday they still hadn't left the campsite. They chewed cold jerky from Pinto's saddle pocket and washed it down with gyp water. "A little coffee wouldn't go bad about now," McGuire confessed at last. "If we had some." He could even recall Cookie's gritty brew and soggy sourdoughs with a rumbling belly.

"Maybe," Pinto said tentatively, "if we was to head back to the herd . . ."

But even with a growling belly, Willie McGuire had his pride. "Take away a man's saddle," he said indignantly, "set him afoot and cinch a cook apron on him! Hell's afire, he couldn't never hold his head up again!"

By midafternoon the dun's hoof was getting no better and their stomachs were no fuller. Willie prowled the creek and shot six times at a cottontail rabbit, and Pinto emptied his revolver at a family of prairie chickens. Both returned to camp empty-handed.

"If Jeremy Hooker knowed how much killin' us is goin' to damage his reputation, maybe he wouldn't bother," Pinto said dryly.

About two hours before sundown they heard the squeak of an ungreased wagon wheel, and before long a heavy Studebaker freighter topped a rise and rattled toward them. "Must be a freighter carryin' goods to one of the ranches over on the Palo Duro," McGuire said, brightening. "Must be carryin' enough grub for a army. Maybe we can get him to make camp with us?"

"Maybe . . ." But Pinto was thinking about what the Circle-M scout had said about wagoners, as well as marshals and stage drivers, being on the lookout for Hooker's assailant. "Might be better," he said cautiously, "to go on bein' hungry awhile longer."

"I been hungry long enough!" McGuire started loping toward the Studebaker, waving both arms and hollering. The wagoner sat erect, his foot on the brake, peering suspiciously at the lumbering figure coming toward him. Then, without warning, he released the brake and whipped his six mules to a reckless gallop. Within a few minutes the freighter had disappeared on the other side of the rise.

Willie McGuire stood stunned in the middle of the prairie, both arms still outraised. "Now why," he asked in amazement, "do you reckon he'd go and do a thing like that?"

Pinto came up behind his partner, and they stood looking at the cloud of dust that the wagon had stirred up. Slowly, Willie let his arms drop to his side. He said, "You figger that wagoner's heard about Jeremy Hooker?"

"That's what I figger," Pinto told him.

"You figger he'll go to Hooker and tell him about seein' us here?"

"He'll tell somebody. Word'll get to Hooker soon enough."

"But it's still too soon for Hooker to ride, with that leg of his."

"He can send a marshal—or somebody—to stop us and hold us."

McGuire concentrated with all his might for

several minutes. He couldn't think of any more arguments. "You don't figger the dun can make it to Chihuahua?"

Pinto looked at him and smiled wanly.

McGuire sighed and grappled with the problem of survival. Leading the dun most of the way, he reckoned that they could overtake the Circle-M herd in about twelve hours. On an empty belly, it was not a pleasant prospect. He shot a pleading look at his partner but Pinto only shook his head.

"Sooner we get started, the better."

It was early morning—the last night watch was just riding out to the herd—when Willie and Pinto finally raised the wagon lantern. They had been traveling for the best part of twelve hours, taking turns at riding Pinto's grulla and leading the dun. They were footsore and empty-gutted and sour with exhaustion. The aroma of coffee lay on the cool air, mingled with dust from the remuda.

They turned their horses into the remuda with the Circle-M animals, and stumbled on to the wagon. A cursing cowhand had just been rousted out of his bed and was building up the fires for the first meal of the day. The time was not quite three o'clock—the beginning of the wagon cook's workday.

Wearily, Willie and Pinto sank to the ground and helped themselves to the coffee. The cowhand with the cook apron tied around his middle dropped his attempt at fire building and looked at them in frank surprise. "The boss said you'd be back before long, but I never believed him." Grinning, he built himself a cigarette and hunkered down to smoke it. "Shorty Eller said you boys was high-tailin' it to the Bravo last time he seen you. What happened?"

"My dun lamed up," Willie told him. "Whereabouts is the boss?"

"Sleepin'. But I'll chance wakin' him up if you're aimin' to put in for the cook job."

McGuire looked as if he were about to sign his own death warrant. Pinto said quickly, "Tell him we're back and ready to work, if the jobs're still open."

They sat staring forlornly into the smoky fire. After a few minutes Arnie Stone came out of the darkness, poured himself some coffee and looked at his two guests. "You boys come back a little quicker'n I figgered you would. Did you run into Jeremy Hooker?"

Pinto spread his arms in an expression of helplessness and told him about the wagoner and the lamed dun. Willie was too overcome by his misfortune to make any comment.

"All right," the boss said briskly. "The cook's job's still open. So's the nighthawk's. It's the nighthawk's duty to swamp for the cook when he ain't with the remuda, help load and unload the wagon, fetch water and wood, wash the dishes and scrub the ovens. You can sleep in the wagon while it's movin' from one place to another."

Pinto nodded wearily. He'd nighthawked on other outfits and knew what kind of job it was. Arnie Stone turned to McGuire. "You think you can keep that temper cinched in and cook three hot meals a day?"

Willie groaned and looked as if he'd rather not think about it. But he nodded.

"Breakfast," Stone warned them, "will be in two hours. You boys better get to rattlin' pans." He turned and marched back to his bed.

After a long, dejected silence, Pinto asked, "Did you ever try cookin' a hot meal for maybe fourteen drovers?"

Willie rose tiredly to the bait, as Pinto hoped he would. "I *seen* it done plenty of times. There ain't nothin' to it. It's the principal of the thing that galls me." He heaved an enormous sigh and shoved himself to his feet. "But I guess we ain't got much say-so about it. If we want to eat, we got to cook." He lit the rear wagon lantern and began poking about in the chuck box. He found the sourdough keg and inspected the eye-watering contents. The yeast was working all right—that was the most important thing on any trail drive. Hot sourdough biscuits, come stampedes, plagues, hell, or highwater. He inspected the lard can. The stores of flour and salt. The sugar and flavorings.

Pinto, rummaging inside the wagon, located

dried apples, Arbuckle's coffee, dry salt pork, a case of canned tomatoes, and two quarters of fresh beef. He handed one quarter of beef down to Willie—any wagon cook that didn't serve fried steak three times a day ran a risk of violent revolution.

Willie had rustled together the outfit's collection of heavy iron skilletlike pans and was regarding them with some dismay. Dutch ovens. Without them a trail outfit would most likely starve, but McGuire had never realized that one wagon would use so many of them. He was beginning to suspect that cooking for a full crew might not be such a simple operation after all.

"The water barrel's most full," Pinto announced, climbing down from the wagon. "We're lucky there. And somebody thought to fill the possum belly with wood the last time they come through a blackjack thicket." He indicated the bulging rawhide fuel container attached to the underside of the wagon. Pinto squinted at his partner who was still staring dejectedly at the array of Dutch ovens. "What's the matter with you?"

"I never figgered there'd be so many damn pans to wrestle all at once! How the hell's a man goin' to grab hold of ever'thing?"

Pinto was powerfully tempted to remind McGuire that he was the one who had made wagon cookery sound so easy, but he bit the words back. "We'll just have to take her a step at a time," he said patiently. "Put our heads together and recollect all the wagon cooks we've seen. First thing to do is build up the fire, so's we'll have a good bed of cookin' coals."

McGuire brightened. Now that he had been shown the right place to begin, his confidence returned. He slapped his big hands together and rubbed them in anticipation. It was all coming back to him now, the dozens of camp and wagon cooks that he had watched at one time or another. The fires, the coffee, the sourdough biscuits, the steaks.

As Pinto added more wood to the fire trench, McGuire located the bread pan and filled it half full of flour. He added some working yeast from the sourdough keg, some salt, some lard, some baking soda. Not too much soda, or the biscuits would turn yellow. He put in enough water to make a dough. McGuire began to whistle tunelessly as he worked. Hell, boys, there ain't nothin' to this cookin', it's just a matter of recollectin' what you seen over the years. Willie even remembered to go to the letdown washstand at the side of the wagon and dip his hands in the water before plunging them into the biscuit dough. Queer thing about cowhands; they could go for weeks without bothering to change their socks, but they demanded cleanliness of the cook. Well, if you're going to do a thing, you might as well do her right.

By the time Willie had his biscuit dough ready Pinto had melted a little lard in each of the Dutch ovens. McGuire squeezed off small bits of dough, coated them with lard and placed them in the ovens to rise. Pinto heaped glowing coals on the oven lids—if the biscuits were to brown properly, the lids had to be good and hot. Even a night-hawk had sense enough to know that.

For some time Willie stood beaming fondly at his lard-coated biscuits, until Pinto reminded him, "Them steaks ain't goin' to cook theirselves." Willie left his biscuits reluctantly, like a mother abandoning her children. There were steaks to be cut, then pounded with the broad side of a hatchet until they promised to be reasonably tender. The pounded steaks were dredged in flour and stacked on the tailgate of the wagon which was also the cook table and the lid to the chuck box.

Pinto made fresh coffee in the time-honored method of the Southwest. Throw several handfuls of coffee into the wide-bottomed pot, wet it down with a little water and boil it until it was stout enough to float a horseshoe, as the saying went. While the coffee boiled, Pinto raked the coals and began frying suet in the steak skillets—no self-respecting cowhand would eat beefsteak fried in lard.

The routine which had begun leisurely with Willie's manufacture of the sourdoughs had steadily increased in tempo until, by the time the steaks were ready to be fried, both men were snarling and cursing, juggling hot ovens and skillets in a frenzy of action. The steaks were dropped into the sizzling fat and cooked well done. More hot coals were piled on the oven lids and the sourdoughs put on to cook.

In the magical way of all wagon cooks, even the worst ones, the meal was somehow, no matter how poorly done, ready in time. Willie and Pinto sagged against the side of the wagon catching their breaths. Wearily, they looked at themselves, grease-spattered, scorched, scalded, dripping with sweat and shaky with exhaustion . . . and the day's work was just beginning. After the morning meal there would be dishes to be washed, equipment to be packed and the wagon to be moved to the next campsite. "By God," Willie McGuire grinned weakly to his partner, "I *told* you there wasn't nothin' to this cookin' business!"

Moving deliberately, McGuire brushed himself off, wiped his sweaty face on his sleeve, walked out a few paces from the wagon and bellowed into the before-dawn darkness, "Come and get it before I throw it to the hogs!"

From a dozen different parts of the prairie drovers began crawling out of their blankets, like huge moths breaking free of their cocoons. The darkness was punctuated by a dozen little lights as the men lit their first smokes of the day. When they finished their smokes they rolled their beds and started toward the wagon.

With a jurylike air they stood around the fire, moving one at a time to the tailgate to draw their eating irons. They began helping themselves to the steak and biscuits and coffee. Willie suddenly remembered he had forgotten to salt the meat, but he decided not to correct the oversight, as such action might suggest to the drovers that the breakfast was less than perfect.

The biscuits, as seen with an objective eye, were clearly burned at the bottom and improperly browned on top. Also, they lay in the bottom of the oven, flat and heavy, clear indication that the cook had not crowded them in close enough when he had set them out to rise. Too, there was a curious odor to the biscuits when they were broken apart, and the inside was an unmistakable yellow instead of the desired snowy white. Despite his care, too much soda had somehow found its way into the dough. McGuire scowled and glared at his partner, as if the error had been Pinto's.

"Godamighty!" a cowhand muttered as he bit into one of the sourdoughs.

Willie stepped toward him, with a pothook in his hand. "You got a complaint to make about the grub?"

"Now that you mention it," the hand told him bitterly, "there *is* a little somethin'. A goddamn coyote would bust his jaw tryin' to chew this steak. And these sourdoughs would choke a buzzard."

McGuire reached out with a ham-sized hand and seized the drover by his shirt front. He began shaking him in the coldly impersonal way of a terrier shaking a rat. The startled cowhand's teeth began to rattle. He dropped his breakfast on the coffee fire. His eyes bulged as Willie twisted the shirt at his throat and shut off his breathing. He began making strange sounds.

"That'll do," a voice said quietly. Arnie Stone stepped into the circle of firelight.

"You got a complaint to make?" Willie asked the trail boss while still shaking the drover.

"No complaints, McGuire," Stone went on with studied calm. "But there's a jug of lick in the wagon somewheres—maybe the boys would like some of it on their biscuits."

Willie appeared almost disappointed that the boss hadn't tried to make a fight of it. But he shrugged and released the drover who fell back in the shadows gasping for breath. Pinto, appreciating the boss's show of self-control, quickly climbed into the wagon and found the jug of black molasses. The rest of the drovers, taking their lead from the boss, silently lined up at the rear of the wagon and drowned their heavy biscuits with the black sweetening.

The meal was finished quickly in a strained

silence. One by one the men stepped up to the wagon, dropped their dishes into the wreck pan and went to get their horses for the day's work. There was a pale streak of light along the eastern horizon, but the sun had not yet made an appearance.

Arnie Stone, the last to leave, dropped his dishes in the pan. "McGuire," he said wearily, "I need a cook, and you need the protection of the outfit. That may not be the best way to run the headquarters wagon, but it's what we're stuck with. It's a big herd, and a long way to Dodge—we've got to come to an understandin'. Can I trust you to run the wagon and get the meals ready on time, or am I goin' to have to let you go and put one of my regular hands to cookin'?"

They looked each other over carefully, like strange dogs meeting on a narrow path. In size and strength they were almost a perfect match. McGuire thoughtfully scratched his bristling chin. "You never said how you liked the breakfast."

"The biscuits was soggy and the steak was flat, but I figger you can learn."

Pinto closed his eyes and groaned inwardly. But McGuire, unpredictable as ever, suddenly grinned. "I'll run the wagon for you. For a while, anyways."

After Stone had ridden off to the herd, Pinto looked at his partner with ever-growing wonder. "I'm glad you decided to be reasonable for once."

"Reason never had anything to do with it," McGuire said mildly. "Tell you the honest truth, I'm just too wore out to fight right now."

The wagoner, whose name was Horace Root, reported his sighting of McGuire to the rancher whose merchandise he was freighting. The rancher told his foreman who told a hostler in Tar City. By noon of the following day Marshal Frank Hargarty had reported the news to Jeremy Hooker.

Hooker savagely scratched the itching cast on his leg and glared at the town from his hotel window. "There can't be any mistake about this? The wagoner's sure it was McGuire?"

"He fit McGuire's description. And he had a sidekick with him that sounds like Gonzales."

The gunman turned to the marshal and smiled like a steel trap snapping shut. "I want all roads watched. All towns and settlements."

"That's not an easy order."

"I won't be an easy man to live with if you let them get away." He thought for a moment, his eyes gray and distant. "Go down to the wagon yard, find the liveryman and send him here. And I want to talk to a caprenter."

"A carpenter?"

The gunslinger again showed his steely smile. "Do like I say, Marshal, and by this time tomorrow I'll be out of Tar City."

The liveryman and the carpenter were sent to Hooker's room. The gunman explained what he wanted and they immediately set about satisfying his wishes.

"Tell that sawbones doc I want to see him. What's his name?"

"Doc Wilford Mulley," the hotel owner said with trembling deference.

"Tell him that Jeremy Hooker wants him. Tell him to jump."

The hotel owner scurried into the streets looking for the doctor. Within fifteen minutes Wilford Mulley was standing in the gunslinger's room. "Much as I hate to," the killer said dryly, "I aim to leave this little city of yours, Mulley."

The doc frowned. "It would be dangerous tryin' to ride, the shape your leg's in."

"I don't aim to try settin' a saddle yet. But is there any reason why I can't drive a buggy?"

The little doc blinked his watery eyes. "I guess not. With the plaster of paris, and the right kind of support for your leg."

The gunman showed him a row of sharklike teeth. "Go down to the livery barn and show the liveryman and the carpenter how the buggy's to be fixed. And Doc . . ."

Mulley was easing nervously out of the room. He came to a trembling halt. ". . . Yes?"

"I'm puttin' it in your hands, Doc. If anything goes wrong, I'll kill you."

Early that afternoon a very nervous liveryman returned to the killer's hotel room. "Mr. Hooker, I'm scared we've run into a little piece of trouble. The buggy . . . the one that we was fixin' up for you? It's already been rented."

Hooker barely bothered to glance at him. "Unrent it."

"Yes sir." Fat beads of sweat were forming on the liveryman's heavy jowls. "That's just what I aim to do. But she's makin' such a fuss about it, on account of she paid for it in advance a week ago, by mail."

"She?" Hooker asked with little interest.

"Yes sir, a widow woman. Missus Ellie Moncrief. Her husband, Ab Moncrief, used to run the Circle-M outfit down below the Cap Rock. Missus Moncrief runs it now. Ab's horse fell on him two, three years ago. He lingered that summer and finally died of the lung fever."

"What does she want the buggy for?"

"Well, she's sendin' a bunch of beef up the trail to Dodge. The herd's over to the east of here somewheres, and she claims she has to get to it and talk to her trail boss."

"Set her up in another rig."

"Yes sir, I thought about that." The liveryman looked as if he might burst into tears. "But she won't listen. She says the buggy's hers and she aims to use it come hell or high water."

Hooker had all but put the matter from his mind.

He was about to tell the liveryman to get out and leave him alone—then a thought occurred to him. "Where did you say that herd is?"

"Over to the east somewhere, on the Western Trail."

The gunman did some silent calculations. McGuire and Gonzales had been to the south, not far off the cattle trail, when the wagoner had spotted them. That would put them within an easy day's ride of the herd. Frowning, Hooker tried to put himself in McGuire's boots. What would he do if he wanted to leave the country and knew that all exits were being watched? Hide himself in a big herd moving north? Surround himself with armed drovers? Why not? It wouldn't be the first time that a hunted man had managed to escape under the protection of a trail outfit.

"You tell the widow I'm headed that way myself, soon as the buggy gets fixed up. Tell her I'll be proud to take her with me, if she don't mind a little company."

The liveryman looked at him in surprise. "That's right gentlemanly of you, Mr. Hooker. I'll go tell Missus Moncrief."

The liveryman clattered out of the room and down the stairs.

The gunman sat for a long while in front of the open window. The more he thought about it the surer he was that McGuire and Gonzales had hooked up with the herd. The irony of the situation caused him to smile. "Right obligin' of you, Missus Moncrief," he said dryly to the empty room. "The boss woman ridin' right beside me, right up to the headquarters wagon—it's like bein' handed a free ticket to McGuire's funeral."

three

His first day as wagon cook was not one that McGuire and Pinto would soon forget. They heated water, washed the tin breakfast dishes with lye soap and put them away. They washed the ovens and skillets and scoured them with sand. In the far distance—almost in another world, it seemed—the drovers were getting the cattle pointed north. Two hands brought up the outfit's four mules and hooked them up to the wagon—hooking up his own team was something a wagon cook never stooped to. The scout, Shorty Eller, grudgingly gave them a hand with loading the bedrolls and gave them directions to the next campsite.

"Watch out for cut banks and dog holes. There's a wash, maybe a mile to the west, but the bottom's solid and the water's low. You won't have no trouble crossin'."

McGuire grunted wearily and eyed the burning sun that was just beginning to rise. Pinto emptied the coffeepot on the fire—the last thing to be done when breaking camp. At last they climbed into the wagon and pointed the mules north.

They circled around the slow-moving herd and rapidly left it behind. In a few minutes they were all alone—or seemed to be—on the open prairie.

McGuire looked at his partner and said worriedly, "By God, this ain't no more protection than we had when we was all to ourselves!"

But Pinto pointed to a distant figure of a horseman—the scout or one of the point riders—on a distant ridge. He rode along that bit of high ground for several minutes, watching the wagon, assuring himself that it was safe and pointed in the right direction. McGuire felt a little better—but not much. In case of emergency, help was still a long way off.

The July sun climbed the eastern sky and the prairie shimmered. Gonzales, knowing that he had a sleepless night ahead of him, climbed into the back of the wagon, wedged himself in among the bedrolls and supplies and tried to rest. Toward midmorning Arnie Stone rode in from a scout and filled his canteen from the wagon's water barrel.

"If you see a buggy over in that direction . . ." He pointed generally to the west. ". . . Most likely it'll be Missus Moncrief. Just tell her to stay with the wagon till the herd catches up, and I'll talk to her then."

That the trail boss apparently expected to see a woman appear suddenly on the bald prairie, in a buggy, was a startling notion to McGuire. "Who's this Missus Moncrief?"

"Owner of the Circle-M. Widow of Ab Moncrief that died three years ago." With a curt little nod, the trail boss jerked his hat down on his forehead and spurred back to the herd.

The wagon jolted along for several minutes over ruts and outcrops as Willic McGuirc dwcllcd on the wonder of the thing. "Gonzales!" he suddenly yelled. "Did you hear that? By God, we went and signed on with a outfit that's got a *woman* for a boss!"

Pinto groaned groggily as the wagon struck another outcrop. "I heard. Try to be a little more careful where you're goin'!"

"A *woman!*" Willie repeated indignantly. Not, of course, that he had anything against women as such; his weakness for trim ankles and pretty faces was notorious in trail town saloons. But a woman *boss* was an entirely different matter. Hard luck was the best you could expect from such an outfit—as any seaman who'd ever sailed with a woman on board could tell you. "And hard luck," Willie thought ruefully, "is somethin' I could do without right now."

The "wash" that the scout had mentioned in such an offhand manner, turned out to be a full-sized creek, and the "solid bottom" turned out to be a treacherous trap of boggy mud and tangled cedar roots. Pinto dragged himself groggily out of the wagon and hacked the wheels free of the roots. "It's already started," McGuire moaned, high and dry on the wagon seat.

"What's already started?" Pinto asked dazedly.

"Hard luck. If I'd knowed this was a she-run outfit I never would of hired on."

Pinto shook his head in profound disinterest and climbed back into the wagon. Within seconds, wet and muddy, he had wedged himself in between the sacked Arbuckle's and the bedrolls, his eyes glazed, his ears totally deaf to his partner's complaining.

It was almost time for the noonday meal when the mules dragged the wagon to the bald knoll that Stone had chosen for the midday campsite. Methodically, McGuire turned the wagon into the wind. Pinto dragged himself out of the wagon and mutely began digging the fire trenches. Two hands from the herd rode in and unhitched the team.

"The boss'll raise pure hell," one of the grinning drovers told McGuire, "if there ain't plenty of grub, and on time." Wisely, he spurred away before McGuire could reach him.

The realization of all the work that must be done struck Willie McGuire with a numbing force. He was sorely tempted to pull his dun out of the remuda, ride away from the outfit and let the cowhands feed themselves for a change.

But even a wagon cook had his pride. Once he signed on with an outfit he didn't walk off the job just because the going got tough. Not, if he was any good. And besides, there was still the matter of Jeremy Hooker.

McGuire shrugged resignedly, pulled down the

lid of the chuck box and began making his sourdoughs. This time he kept the soda down to a few pinches and added a little sugar to help the biscuits in browning. While he put the sourdoughs aside to rise, Pinto built a roaring fire, put on the coffee and began heating the oven lids.

Willie eyed the beef anxiously as he unwrapped it. As every cowhand knew, fresh beef was set out at night to chill in the cool night air, and during the day it was kept in the wagon out of the sun. Willie had forgotten to set it out. It was beginning to smell a little "high," and there were some faintly disturbing spots of green beginning to form on the cut surfaces. McGuire sighed, sharpened his knife and cut off the offending spots. He would add plenty of pepper. Maybe no one would notice.

Once again the work tempo, which had started at a leisurely pace, mounted to a barely controlled frenzy at the approach of high noon. The biscuits had to be watched to make sure that they were browning and not burning. The suet had to be rendered and the steaks pounded and floured and fried. It was Pinto's job to see that the cooking coals were kept alive and that the coffeepot was full. All this beneath a blistering July sun, while a fitful wind showered the prepared food with sand and gravel.

To Willie's surprise the first batch of steaks and biscuits were ready to set off the fire as the first shift of drovers rode in from the herd. In a sudden fit of goodwill McGuire added flour and water and salt to the steak fat and stirred up a batch of gravy.

The first hand to fill his plate sniffed the steaks suspiciously. However, tainted steaks were not unusual on a long drive; fresh meat did not last long in the July heat, and cattlemen were notoriously reluctant to kill their own beef. The hand speared several biscuits on his fork, ladled some gravy over them and found a place on the lee of the wagon to sit.

Willie watched him expectantly. The drover bit into one of the biscuits, cut himself a piece of steak and chewed thoughtfully, ignoring the fine coating of sand. After his first mouthful he looked at McGuire in surprise. The sourdoughs, with the help of a little sugar, had browned evenly on top. The bottoms were crisp but not burned, the insides chewy but not tough. The steaks were properly salted and peppered and pounded to chewability—no reasonable cowhand would complain that the smell was a little "high."

The hand bit into another biscuit and chewed with appreciation. He looked at McGuire and said, "These here sourdoughs ain't half bad . . ." Willie beamed. A wagon cook survived or fell on his reputation for cooking sourdoughs. Then the drover ruined everything and added, ". . . Cookie."

McGuire stood for a moment, a half smile frozen on his craggy face. The time, he realized, had come for an understanding with the outfit. His own peculiar position with the herd needed to be explained in terms that even the dullest mind could understand.

Gonzales was making strange little sounds in his throat while striving to signal his partner with his eyes. McGuire ignored him. He stepped across the coffee fire, pushed up his sleeves and stood towering over the startled cowhand. "The name ain't Cookie," he said with an unhappy little grin. "And it ain't Belly-cheater, or Dough-wrangler, or Greasy-belly, or Grub-spoiler, or none of them other names that some wagon cooks is known by. It's McGuire. Nothin' else—just McGuire."

The intimidated cowhand stared up at Willie McGuire's huge frame and quickly decided not to take offense. Instead, he wisely saluted the cook with one of his biscuits and, after clearing his throat, said weakly, "These here sourdoughs ain't half bad . . . McGuire."

"Help yourself," McGuire said happily, as though nothing had happened. "There's plenty for ever'body."

After an uneven start at breakfast, the noon meal was—in McGuire's mind, at least—a great success. The hands had eaten the food with a minimum of fuss, and Willie had established himself as the boss of the wagon.

After the second shift of drovers had eaten and returned to the herd, Willie and Pinto once again began the never-ending job of cleaning up and breaking camp. Arnie Stone rode in from the herd to help hitch up the mules. "Don't forget to keep a sharp watch for that buggy," he reminded them.

Willie regarded the lines of concern about the eyes of the trail boss. "I forgot to ask—what's a woman doin' out on the prairie by herself, anyhow?"

It was not the trail boss's duty to explain himself to the wagon cook. He only shrugged, while studying the western horizon. "I told you, she owns the Circle-M."

"But you're the trail boss. Is she scared you can't get the herd to Dodge by yourself?"

Stone turned and looked at McGuire without expression. "It's beginnin' to look like you might have the makin's of a wagon cook, McGuire. Most likely we'll get along . . . if you keep one thing in mind. I'm the boss, and I don't like the hands meddlin' in my personal affairs." With a curt nod, he stepped into the stirrup and headed back to the herd.

Willie McGuire stared in amazement. "Now what do you reckon *that* was all about?"

"Sounded plain enough to me," Pinto told him. "He don't want folks buttin' in on his private business."

McGuire thought about this for a moment. "You figger he's went and got hisself cow-eyed over that widow woman?"

"That's what I figger." Pinto smiled. "But I don't aim to ask him about it."

For the second time that day they packed the wagon and drowned the fires and headed toward the new campsite four miles north of the herd. "Don't hardly seem like we're with a cow outfit at all," Willie said, as the wagon jolted from one outcrop to another. "About all we ever see of the herd is a cloud of dust over on the far rise, and sometimes you can't even see that. For a hand that don't much like the sight of cows, I guess the wagon's the place to be."

Pinto made no answer. He had again wedged himself in among the bedrolls and was fitfully sleeping as the wagon reeled and jolted across the prairie.

The new campsite was on a small, brackish stream, the banks sparsely studded with cottonwood and salt cedar. Bedground for the cattle had been established downstream, almost half a mile from the wagon. Willie wrapped the lines and wearily climbed down from the wagon seat. "Rise and shine!" he hollered to his partner. "This here's our new home."

Pinto, roused from the only sleep he would get before taking up his duties as nighthawk, climbed groggily down to the ground and began digging the fire trenches. "At least there's some firewood," he said. "And water—if it's fit to drink."

"It's fit to drink," Willie said confidently, "or

the boss wouldn't of brought the cattle to it." Rummaging in the grub box he discovered a second bottle of lemon extract. "Well, now," he murmured happily, uncorking the bottle and helping himself to a generous pull. "Say what you will, but bein' a wagon cook has its advantages."

After a second pull at the extract bottle the world became a considerably brighter place to live in. Exhaustion fell away like scales from a shedding snake. McGuire rubbed his hands together with a new briskness, hitched up his pants and called to his partner, "Gonzales, didn't you locate some dried apples when you were scroungin' around in the wagon last night?"

"Two boxes. About twenty pounds, I guess." Pinto, downwind from McGuire, raised his head and sniffed. "The boss'll have your hide if he catches you in the extract."

"The boss is just about to find out how lucky he is that Willie McGuire decided to hook up with his outfit. Break out the dried apples, Gonzales, we're goin' to have fried pies for supper."

Pinto shot him a suspicious glance. "You ever try your hand at cookin' fried pies?"

"Nothin' to it. Seen it done plenty times." McGuire had another go at the extract and reluctantly corked the bottle.

With a look of grave misgiving on his brown face, Pinto climbed into the wagon and handed down the dried apples. McGuire folded his arms

Indian-like across his chest and shut his eyes in fierce concentration. First the apples had to be stewed—he remembered that very well. And there was crust to be made. Lard to be heated in a big Dutch oven. Put the stewed apples in the crust and fry it in the lard. Easy as falling off a green bronc.

Willie measured out several handfuls of dried apples into an iron pot, added water, sugar and a few drops of the precious extract. "And a drop for the cook," he murmured happily to himself, again swigging from the neck of the bottle. He turned the apples over to Pinto. "Soon's the fire burns down and the coals're good'n hot, put these on and let 'em stew."

That took care of the apples. For crust he simply made up an extra batch of biscuit dough. Willie began whistling a lively little tune as he plunged his hands into the dough and gave it a good punching. Two drovers rode in from the herd, unhooked the mules and turned them into the remuda. Helping themselves to coffee, they eyed the stewing apples with suspicious eyes.

"What's that in the pot, McGuire?"

"Never you mind what's in the pot," McGuire said placidly. He made his biscuits, put them in the ovens and set them near the fire to rise. In a separate oven he placed the extra mound of dough. The two drovers looked at each other, shook their heads and returned to the herd.

Willie was happily cutting and pounding steaks

at the letdown table when Pinto called in a strange voice, "McGuire, you better come here a minute."

McGuire put down his hatchet and went to the fire where the apples were stewing. "Hell and damnation!" he said, staring at the writhing mess in the pot. "She's swole up like a muley cow with the bloats!"

They watched mutely as the dried apples increased in size as they absorbed water. It was well known that such things happened with rice, and Southwest humor was rich with yarns of cowcamps that had silently floated away on seas of that boiled grain, but Willie had never heard of it happening with apples.

The bubbling mass was already slithering over the edge of the pot. "Godamighty!" the wagon cook groaned, "she's goin' out of the banks!" He grabbed the pot with an iron hook and pulled it off the fire. After a moment of mute dismay, Willie wheeled on his partner and growled, "Don't stand there like a fencepost, get a shovel and start diggin'!"

As furtively as if they were burying the hide of a stolen calf, Pinto helped McGuire bury his mistake. Well away from the wagon they dug a hole, ladled half the apples into it and covered it. Willie stood glaring down at the patch of raw earth as if it were the grave of a despised enemy. Just when he was feeling confident and secure in his job, a few handfuls of shriveled-up apples showed him up for a fool. No wonder, he thought, that wagon cooks were noted for their bad tempers! The pair returned to the wagon and the incident was never mentioned again.

Pinto watched with a certain fascination as McGuire continued his manufacture of fried pies. First he rolled out some dough, cut some round pieces with a baking powder can and filled the center with stewed fruit. Then he folded the dough over the fruit and dropped it in the oven of hot fat. The circle of dough promptly popped open, the fruit spewed hissing into the bubbling lard, and Willie was ten minutes fishing all the bits and pieces out of the oven.

He finally discovered that the half circle of dough could be sealed with the tines of a fork, and that a few pricked holes in the side of the pie would release pent-up steam. He filled a test pie, sealed it, pricked it and dropped it into the hot lard. It simmered cheerily on the surface of the grease. Willie turned it with a fork and browned it on the other side. "There she is," McGuire said proudly, dishing it onto a plate. "Get yourself a fork, Gonzales, and dig in."

With no great enthusiasm, Pinto got himself a fork, cut off a bite of hot pie and chewed thoughtfully. Surprisingly, it was no worse than other fried pies that he had eaten on other trail drives. Willie grinned with pleasure as his partner, on his own account and without coaxing, cut off another piece and ate it with apparent satisfaction.

Supper that night was a great success. Cow-hands starved for sweets wolfed the tough pies as though they had been the prize efforts of a real baker. Even the boss came back for seconds.

"McGuire . . ."

McGuire folded his arms and waited for his well-deserved praise.

"These pies of yours ain't too hard to choke down, McGuire."

The boss of the wagon—the cook of the Circle-M—beamed.

The next morning at first light the livery buggy pulled out of Tar City. Ellie Moncrief sat rigidly erect on the black leather seat. Beside her, his injured leg resting in a cradle device that the Tar City carpenter had rigged up, sat the gunslinger, Jeremy Hooker. They made a strange pair—Hooker, as dark and deadly as a newly blued pistol; Ellie Moncrief, fair and cool and pleasing to look at without being frail.

Hooker clucked dryly to the livery mare between the shafts. From time to time he would cast a sidelong glance at the Widow Moncrief, and occasionally he would choke down a curse as the buggy lunged from rut to rut along the service road from Tar City. The narrow tires of farmers' "butcher knife wagons" had cut the road into a network of parallel trenches, and it was with relief when Hooker finally pulled off the road and started east across the open prairie.

"With a little luck," the gunman said at last, "we'll be raisin' the herd around dinnertime."

Ellie Moncrief looked straight ahead and said nothing. The last word she had spoken to him had been at the livery barn in Tar City. "This here," the liveryman had explained to Hooker, "is Missus Moncrief, the boss-lady of the Circle-M, that I was tellin' you about." Hooker had looked at her as if she had been a new rifle model that he had never seen before. "Proud to know you, ma'am." "And this here's Mr. Jeremy Hooker," the liveryman continued nervously. Ellie had looked for a moment into those gunmetal eyes and murmured, ". . . Mr. Hooker."

That had been nearly four hours ago.

Ellie Moncrief had recently crossed over to the shady side of thirty, but the Southwest sun had not yet coarsened the fairness of her complexion, nor had it faded the lively blue of her eyes. She did not think of herself as pretty, but she knew that she was attractive to men. For ten years there had been only one man in her life—she hadn't even been aware of the others—but since Ab's death she had felt the eyes of men following her whenever she moved among them.

It had been a strange sensation at first, knowing that men other than her husband found her desirable. There had been a time, at first, when she had been shamed by it. But not anymore. She had come to accept it, even expect it. Now, when Jeremy Hooker showed no interest at all, in a personal way, she found it vaguely disturbing.

She knew, of course, that the man now sitting beside her was *the* Jeremy Hooker. The gunman. The killer. She was not afraid of him, but she instinctively avoided contact with him, as she would avoid contact with a snake. Still, she was grateful to him for driving her out to the herd, for it was important, urgent, that she talk to Arnie Stone and try to get the herd to moving faster.

Finally, out of sheer boredom, Hooker said, "I don't believe the liveryman said just why it was that you wanted to cut off the herd and talk to your foreman."

Ellie hesitated for a moment, then moved her shoulders in the faintest suggestion of a shrug. There was no secret about what she was doing. She couldn't see that it would matter one way or another to Hooker. "Down south," she said, "along the Nueces, there's a big dry-up. Cowmen are startin' to round up their beef and throw them on the market for whatever they can get. It's just beginnin' now, and not all the cowmen are satisfied it's the thing to do. But," she added with conviction, "sooner or later they'll all be forced to it. Cattle can't live without water. Well, when all that stock is put on the market at the same time, you can see what it'll do to the price of beef in Dodge. What we have to do is speed up the herd, even at the risk of runnin' weight off the cattle, and get to Dodge while the prices are still good."

Hooker smiled faintly, appreciating the tough business mind behind the attractive face.

"I'm afraid I made a fuss about the buggy," Ellie told him, "but you can see why it was important to me."

"I see, ma'am," the gunslinger said blandly. "Don't give it another thought. I was comin' this way anyhow."

Hooker did not care about this widow, either as a woman or as a rancher—only as a means of getting at McGuire. There were few things in this world that Jeremy Hooker did care about. What it boiled down to was the image that Hooker had of himself—that was the thing that really mattered. Maybe the only thing. And it was that image that McGuire had tarnished.

He still went pale with rage when he thought of that night in Tar City—Jeremy Hooker being manhandled by an ignorant cowhand. He could hear the laughter now, in the saloons of Ellsworth, Tascosa, Dodge. *Did you hear about Jeremy Hooker lettin' a saddle tramp bust his leg and then ride off, free as air?* That was the kind of talk that made a man look foolish—and fools were not feared, they were laughed at. This was a thing that Hooker could not allow.

Ellie Moncrief had been saying something, but the gunslinger caught only the last few words. ". . . is anything the matter, Mr. Hooker?"

She was looking at him in a strange way. Hooker knew that the rage inside him had distorted his features. By sheer willpower, he made himself relax. "No," he heard himself saying, "everything's fine, ma'am."

And so it was. Within a few hours Willie McGuire would be dead, and his problem would be solved.

four

McGuire's day began, as every wagon cook's day began, several hours before dawn, with the nighthawk shaking him awake. Willie dragged himself out of the wagon where he had made his bed and stared blearily out at the dark prairie. In the distance he could hear the night watch crooning tunelessly to the cattle. Hard work and little rest, long days and short nights. That was the life of every drover, but compared to night-hawking and cooking it was a life of shameful sloth.

Willie got as far as the washstand, splashed a little water on his face, then sat on the ground and began rolling a cigarette. "Gonzales," he said to his partner, "this here ain't no kind of life for a respectable cowhand. First thing after breakfast I aim to tell the boss. We'll draw our time and ride."

"Ride where?"

McGuire made a meaningless gesture. It seemed only minutes ago that he had crawled into the wagon and fallen dead asleep, now it was time to start all over again with getting breakfast. Pinto poured him some coffee from the blackened pot that was never allowed to be cold, except when the wagon was in motion. Somebody from the night watch was always on hand to stir up the coals, or add a little water when the brew had boiled dangerously low.

Willie gulped some coffee and cursed wearily as he burned his mouth on the hot cup. Slowly, he pulled himself to his feet. The morning air was cool and clean. That was something. There was little wind and only minimal dust, which was all to the good. "Goddamn!" he said aloud, "I'm even beginnin' to *think* like a wagon cook! I got to get away from this outfit before I'm marked for life!"

From the rear of the wagon Pinto had unwrapped a forequarter of beef and was sniffing it. "You better get the boss to kill some fresh meat today, this is gettin' pretty ripe." Then he built up the cooking fires and went back to the remuda.

Little by little McGuire got himself moving. Methodically, he drew off the required amount of sourdough batter, refilled the keg with flour and water and began making his biscuit dough. The night before, after the great success of the fried pies, he had felt like the king of the outfit. This morning he doubted that he was even a man. A goddamn dough-puncher, he thought bitterly. That's all I'll ever amount to, long's I stay with this outfit.

Somehow the biscuits had browned and the steaks were ready to take from the skillet as Pinto turned the saddle band over to the day wrangler. "No two ways about it," McGuire vowed, "this here's the last meal I aim to wrangle skillets for. Somebody else can cinch on this cook apron; I aim to head for some high country."

"You signed on for the job," Pinto reminded him. "And it ain't a bad outfit, as trail outfits go. We could do worse."

McGuire snorted. "There ain't no way to do worse than goin' through life with your hands in biscuit dough."

"And then there's Jeremy Hooker," Pinto pointed out. "Most likely his leg's beginnin' to mend by this time."

Willie McGuire glared belligerently at the dark prairie. "Well," he said grudgingly, "maybe I'll finish out the day. Give the boss a chance to break in another hand." He tramped away from the wagon and hollered for the drovers to come and get it.

With the decision made to stay out the day, Willie's fortunes went steadily downhill. What had promised to be a relatively pleasant day for July turned blustery and hot. The wind whipped sand and gravel into the pile of cooked steaks, it laid down a curtain of eye-watering smoke that followed a man with the persistence of a pet colt looking for sugar. On top of that the day wrangler got his foot caught in the stirrup as he was dismounting and badly twisted his ankle. It was the cook's job to do the doctoring and get him back in the saddle at the earliest possible moment.

Willie stared at the swollen ankle which was

already turning blue. With a fatalistic shrug, he dosed it with horse liniment and coal oil, bound it with one of his flour sack dish towels and boosted the wrangler into the wagon.

Arnie Stone stopped by the wagon before riding out to the herd. "Don't forget to keep an eye peeled for that buggy, McGuire."

McGuire stared blankly. He had forgotten that, on top of his other miseries, the outfit's female owner was expected to inspect the herd.

The trail boss pointed toward the west. "Missus Moncrief will be comin' from over there somewheres, from Tar City."

McGuire looked startled. He hadn't realized that the herd had moved that close to the scene of all the unpleasantness—as he liked to think of it. "I thought the outfit's headquarters was down south of the Cap Rock. What's a woman by herself doin' in a place like Tar City?"

"All I know," the trail boss said testily, "is she sent word by a drover's supply man that we was to look for her here." He tugged his hat down on his forehead, irritated at having to explain himself to a common cook. He might have added that Ellie Moncrief usually did as she pleased and asked nobody's advice—but he had already said too much.

Willie stood for some time staring dejectedly toward the west. It wasn't that he was afraid of Hooker—he kept telling himself—it was just that he had never bothered to learn to fire a revolver with any kind of accuracy. Until recently it hadn't seemed important. It had never crossed his mind that one day he might find himself at the top of a gunslinger's hunted list.

The injured day wrangler, a string bean of a man who went by the name of Matchstick, pushed up the wagon sheet and eyed the cook with interest. "How'd you come to bust that gunshark's leg, McGuire?"

McGuire shrugged. "I can't recollect."

"The boys'll look out for you," the wrangler grinned. "Long's the coffee's hot and the biscuits light. And ever' once in a while a batch of them fried pies wouldn't hurt none either."

"I don't need no damn bunch of cow nurses lookin' out for me," McGuire growled. But, as he washed the dishes and began to break camp, he was comforted to see that Stone and one of the swing riders were holding up on a distant ridge to see that the wagon got away safely. As they began moving toward the midday campsite, at least one Circle-M rider remained within rifle shot of the wagon. McGuire, after long consideration, decided that maybe he'd stay on for another day or so as cook. Until he had a little more distance between himself and Tar City, anyhow.

McGuire reached the campsite and turned the wagon into the wind. Pinto, who had been sleeping in the depth of the wagon, dragged himself up to the driver's seat and gazed groggily out at the brown prairie. In the distance a single rider was watching the wagon; the herd itself was not in sight.

The buggy first appeared as a small black dot on a distant rise. It dipped into a shallow fold of the prairie and disappeared for several minutes. When it reappeared, it was much closer.

After a stretch of silence, Pinto said quietly, "McGuire, you reckon that's the boss woman that Stone said to look out for?"

"I reckon we'll know before long."

The buggy stopped for a moment on a ridge and they saw that there was a second figure sitting beside the driver.

"McGuire . . ." Pinto said worriedly. "It's the gunslinger."

McGuire nodded heavily. "I can see him."

Matchstick crawled up from the belly of the wagon and stared in awe at the distant buggy. "Is it actually Jeremy Hooker?"

"Busted leg and all," McGuire groaned. "He must be pretty sore, to come all this way in a buggy, with his leg done up in a cast like that."

"What do you aim to do if he starts toward the wagon?"

"I sure don't aim to sit here on this wagon seat like no clay duck in a shootin' gallery,"

McGuire said with feeling. In an amazingly short time he had vacated the seat and had disappeared into the bowels of the wagon.

From a distance of almost half a mile Jeremy Hooker watched the confusing movement of figures in the chuck wagon. "Is that your head-quarters wagon, ma'am?"

Ellie Moncrief nodded.

"What's the name of your cook?"

"I don't know. Wagon cooks come and go."

The gunslinger smiled. "I guess." He clucked to the mare and the buggy began quartering across the prairie, heading toward the wagon. Off to the east a Circle-M rider appeared atop a knoll and sat for some time watching the buggy. Hooker saw the rider, but his presence did not bother him. Nothing could bother him, now that he had McGuire almost in his sights.

After a while a second rider appeared beside the first, and Ellie smiled faintly as she recognized the big fairhaired figure of Arnie Stone. "There's my trail boss," she told the gunman. "I expect he'll meet us at the wagon."

Hooker carefully adjusted his small revolver in his pocket holster so that the gunbutt hooked to the right, the classic position for a crossarm draw. The position a man would take who intended to shoot while sitting.

Ellie regarded him with a growing anxiety.

She had been so intent on reaching the herd herself that she hadn't bothered to wonder about Hooker's reason for coming. "Mr. Hooker," she began slowly, "I don't know what you expect to find here, but maybe I'd better warn you that my drovers are loyal and well armed . . ."

"Shut up," the gunman told her.

Ellie blinked in surprise. The gunslinger had spoken without looking at her, spoken flatly, without emotion, the way he might have spoken to a barking dog. It had been a long time since the mistress of the Circle-M had been spoken to in such a manner. "Do you realize who you're talkin' to . . ."

"Be quiet," he told her again, in the same tone. "From here on out I'll do the talkin'. You sit where you are and behave, and it might be you'll come out of this alive."

The two Circle-M riders were slanting down the grassy slope toward the wagon—they would reach it about the same time the buggy did. Ellie glanced at them, with a growing coldness in the pit of her stomach. She stared at Hooker as though he had suddenly grown a second head. The trip from Tar City had not been unpleasant. The gunman had been cool and distant, but until this moment he had not shown his real face.

"I'm goin' to circle around in front of the mules," he told her now. "Sit still. Don't move unless I tell you."

"What do you intend to do?" She tried to sound indignant, but the words came out pale and weak. "What do you want?"

"I want you to be quiet," he said coldly. He brought the buggy around in front of the wagon. Matchstick, who had taken the lines, nervously hauled the mules to a stop. "Looky here, mister," the wrangler blurted, "that ain't a very smart thing to do, with four spooky mules hooked up to a heavy wagon . . ."

Hooker looked up at Matchstick with those gunmetal eyes, and the wrangler broke off abruptly, as if he had been shot. Arnie Stone and his scout, Shorty Eller, rode up to the wagon. Stone looked worriedly at his boss. He started to get down, but Hooker said, "Stay in the saddle, wagon boss, and do like I say."

Ellie shot a look at Stone, silently asking him to do as the gunman commanded. Stone noted the position of the gunman's revolver, and the picture began taking shape in his mind. "What do you want, Hooker?"

The gunslinger smiled, pleased that he had been recognized. "What I want is simple. A few days back a drifter hooked up with your outfit, name of McGuire. I want him."

Stone raised his arm and wiped a bead of sweat from his forehead. "I don't know anybody named McGuire. And if I did, I wouldn't turn him over to you."

"You know him, and you'll turn him over to me." He looked directly up into Stone's eyes. "Or I'll kill the widow woman."

There was an electric silence. Even the horses stood perfectly still, their heads cocked expectantly. Then there was a sudden rustling inside the wagon. McGuire threw back the canvas sheet and stood up.

All eyes turned to the big figure standing behind the driver's seat. They stared in surprise and perhaps disbelief—but the most surprised person of all was McGuire himself. He hadn't meant to reveal himself, deliberately inviting a bullet from Jeremy Hooker. He had acted without thinking. That was the way it had always been with Willie McGuire.

Hooker looked up at that long, homely face and smiled with immense satisfaction. "I've been waitin' a long spell for this moment, McGuire." He gestured languidly with one hand. "Get yourself a gun, Cookie. I don't want it said that Jeremy Hooker never gave a man an even chance."

McGuire flushed scarlet, grabbed off his floursack apron and hurled it to the gound. "The name ain't Cookie," he told Hooker angrily. "It's McGuire, and don't you forget it."

"Now look here . . ." Arnie Stone started to object.

But McGuire stopped him with an angry bellow. "No sir, by God. He come lookin' for a fight, and he's goin' to find one. Let the woman go, Hooker."

"Just as soon as you get your gun," Hooker said softly.

Inside the wagon Pinto Gonzales groaned to himself. McGuire was playing perfectly into the gunman's hands. Hot with anger, and reckless in the presence of a pretty female, McGuire was completely forgetting the indisputable fact that he was one of the worst pistol shots in Texas.

McGuire, continuing to growl and bellow, climbed down over the front wheel, stomped to the chuck box and hauled out his holstered .45. He blew a cloud of flour and dust from the slightly rusty weapon and began buckling the belt around his middle. "All right," he hollered at the gunman, "I've got me a pistol now."

"So I see," Hooker said with his steely smile. This would make the killing legal. No matter that a gun in the hands of Willie McGuire was no more deadly than a small rock, the fact that McGuire was armed at all would clear Hooker in any court in Texas. "All right, ma'am," he said to Ellie Moncrief. "You can get out of the buggy now."

Ellie got numbly down from the buggy. This thing that was happening—she could see it happening, but she couldn't believe it. It was so senseless. One of the men she didn't know at all, and the other she had known only a short time.

Yet it seemed that somehow, because of her, one of those men was about to kill the other.

Willie, still red-faced and blustery—but most of all angry at being called Cookie—tramped up to the buggy in a curious slope-shouldered crouch that he believed was the correct stance for a lightning-fast gunslinger. Hooker, by contrast, sat relaxed in the buggy, his injured leg wedged into the makeshift cradle, his hands resting carelessly on the leather seat.

"Any time you're ready," Hooker said mildly, "make your draw, McGuire. I wouldn't want it said that Jeremy Hooker took advantage."

Suddenly McGuire pulled up short. Fantasy fled. The reality of the situation struck him with brutal force. He looked into those cool gray eyes and abruptly realized what a fool he was being. He knew that he looked ridiculous, and he felt ridiculous. He was also scared. A little droplet of sweat gathered between his shoulders and slipped down the center of his back like the cut of a knife.

Hooker never changed expression. That supremely confident smile never flickered. Inside the wagon Pinto and Matchstick were as silent as corpses. Arnie Stone stared at the gunslinger with a kind of fatalistic fascination, and Shorty Eller regarded McGuire with a confusion of emotions. Ellie Moncrief looked as if she might start screaming out of sheer frustration, but an icy glance from the gunslinger silenced her immediately.

After what seemed hours of silence, Jeremy Hooker, with all the patience in the world, said again, "Make your draw, McGuire." He thought of something that amused him, and his smile widened. "I'm beginning to think you've got more grit in your sourdough keg than you've got in your craw."

Almost of its own will, Willie's hand started for his .45. Hooker didn't move. He didn't even blink. Clearly, he meant to let McGuire actually make his draw before he moved. With his hand a bare inch from the butt of his revolver, McGuire realized what was happening and froze. An erratic wind whipped sand and fine gravel against the side of the buggy. In McGuire's ears it sounded like a volley of Gatling guns.

McGuire realized that he could wait no longer. He either had to draw or turn tail and run. But he couldn't make up his mind to do either. To act one way would be shameful, to do the other would be suicidal. For several long seconds all he could do was to stand there, awkwardly crouched, and sweat.

McGuire felt that his clothing was soaked with sweat. His palms were wet with it. Great beads of it stood out on his face.

"Well, McGuire?" Hooker asked patiently. He was enjoying his victim's agony of decision.

In the back of his mind McGuire heard the prairie wind flapping the wagon sheet. The mules began to stomp restlessly. The little bay mare between the buggy shafts hunched nervously before another peppering of sand and gravel. Hooker blinked for just a moment as the sand whipped across his face. Willie realized that his time had come.

In a kind of wild despair he grabbed for his .45. As Hooker was blinking, McGuire fumbled the handle of the weapon. In dismay he saw the revolver clattering to the ground and, as he could think of nothing else to do, he dived for it.

Hooker, even in his instant blindness, was completely confident and unruffled. Even while his eyes were closed, his hand snapped effortlessly to his revolver. He fired with the same fluid ease two shots right through the space that McGuire had occupied only an instant before diving after his pistol.

Willie was fumbling beneath the mare's hoofs for his .45 as Hooker's second shot crashed through empty space. The startled mare reared suddenly, terrified at the racket of the shooting and McGuire pawing the ground at its hoofs. The animal's forefeet came down with a crash, inches from McGuire's head. The frightened bay lunged forward in the shafts and the buggy veered toward the wagon.

What happened next was recorded in McGuire's mind in a series of nightmare flashes. Mare and buggy careened toward the wagon. Hooker left the buggy. He took to the air, flapping his arms wildly, like a gorged turkey buzzard trying to get off the ground. The gunslinger flew perhaps a dozen feet before crashing to the prairie. His pistol flew out of his hand and landed near Ellie Moncrief. He hit the ground hollering obscenities at McGuire. He went on hollering for several minutes, until McGuire picked himself up and brushed himself off.

The first frenzy of Hooker's rage soon burned itself out. Suddenly he lay back on the ground, gritting his teeth in pain, and it was then that McGuire noticed the odd angle at which the gunman's injured leg was bent.

An alarming number of things seemed to be happening at the same time. Pinto and Matchstick were scrambling down from the wagon. Shorty Eller was racing after the buggy. Arnie Stone had quietly dismounted and had one arm around Ellie Moncrief. Ellie did not look as if she needed the support; she held Hooker's revolver steadily in both hands, pointed directly at the gunman. As if by magic, several Circle-M hands appeared on a rise and came racing toward the wagon. In the middle of all this activity McGuire stood mute and deaf, aware only of himself and Hooker.

He walked over to the gunslinger and, with an air of resignation, said, "Your leg's busted again, looks like."

Hooker killed him a hundred times with his blazing eyes. "I'll get you, McGuire! Don't you never think I won't! I'll kill you an inch at a time! I'll . . ." The words broke off in a groan of pain. He closed his eyes tightly so that he wouldn't have to look at McGuire. "I want a doc. Send one of the riders to Tar City and tell Doc Mulley to get hisself here in a hurry!"

"Well now," Willie said thoughtfully, "as wagon cook I do what doctorin' that has to be done around here."

"Touch me," the gunman grated, "and I'll kill you with my bare hands!"

McGuire shrugged, stood up and walked over to the trail boss. "It's up to you. If you can spare a hand to go after the doc . . ." For the first time Willie noticed how young Arnie Stone was. Young and inexperienced. There were still some things about trail drives that he didn't know about, and dealing with killers like Jeremy Hooker was one of them.

Arnie took out his bandanna and wiped his face and appeared to be thinking hard. "What do you think, McGuire?"

"Tell you the truth," McGuire answered in all honesty, "I'd just as soon have him away from here. I'd send the hand."

The trail boss wiped his face again. Then he signaled to Shorty Eller and called, "Ride over to Tar City and fetch the doc."

Ellie Moncrief shot her trail boss a little sizing-up look, almost as though she were seeing him for the

90

first time. "Hadn't you better send the hands back to the herd, Arnie? The trouble's over now. It's important that we keep the cattle moving. That's what I came out here to tell you about."

Stone gazed around and looked surprised to see a half dozen excited drovers gathered about the wagon. "The trouble's all over now," he snapped. "Get back to the herd and keep it movin'." He looked at Willie. "Can you make dinner here, where the wagon stands?"

"If the boys don't mind the extra ride to get to it." As a matter of fact McGuire was glad to have the work to look forward to. The numbness following the excitement was beginning to desert him. There was a queasiness in the pit of his stomach when he thought about the gunfight—or what almost had been a gunfight. He had the uneasy feeling that at any moment his hands would start trembling and he wouldn't even be fit for cooking sourdoughs and steaks.

Almost an hour had passed since the drovers had returned to the herd. Pinto had dug the trenches and built the fires and Willie was methodically pounding steaks. Hooker had been hauled up to the shade of the wagon; he now lay with eyes shut tight and jaws clamped.

"You don't look like a wagon cook, McGuire," Ellie Moncrief said. "How'd you come to take this job?"

As he rendered suet and dredged the steaks in flour, Willie told her how he and Pinto had fallen into their jobs. "You mean," she said incredulously, "that you're the one that busted Jeremy Hooker's leg the *first* time?" Suddenly she laughed. It was a loud, silver sound. A man's laughter, but in a higher register. "Now I understand why he was mad enough to kill you." Suddenly she eyed the gunslinger and became thoughtful. "What'll you do now? He'll come after you, soon's his leg mends again."

"I know," Willie sighed.

The noontime meal was always a silent, hurried affair. But today, with Jeremy Hooker balefully glaring at every drover face that appeared in the grub line, the meal was less comfortable than usual. There was sand in the gravy, the biscuits were improperly browned, the steaks were tough. The cowhands sat hunched over on the lee of the wagon, the sun beating down on them as they gulped their food.

Suddenly the gunslinger raised up on his elbows, glared at them and said, "There's one thing you better know, all of you. My business with this grub-burner ain't finished. I'll be comin' after him again, and I'll get him, don't fret yourselves about that." His slitted eyes grew hot. "And I'd take it mighty unfriendly for any man to hinder me in what I've got to do."

All hands stopped in midair. All jaws that had been working methodically on the tough steaks, froze. All eyes fixed on the gunslinger.

"That's how it is," Hooker told them through gritted teeth. "Unless you're anxious to make an enemy out of Jeremy Hooker, you'd be smart to quit this outfit and stay away from the wagon cook."

Ellie Moncrief, who had been observing the scene from the letdown table where she was eating, reacted angrily. "That's enough of that kind of talk, Hooker!"

Hooker turned his head and smiled at her. It was a chilling expression. "If you try to protect that cook, this herd will never get north of the Cimarron."

Willie McGuire felt a little like a corpse, with old acquaintances and enemies talking back and forth across the body as they laid it out. For a moment nobody moved. Then, one by one, the drovers got to their feet, dropped their dishes into the wreck pan and rode back to the herd.

". . . Never get north of the Cimarron," Hooker grated again, looking at the mistress of the Circle-M. Then he closed his eyes and didn't speak again until that afternoon.

Doc Mulley arrived, in the company of Marshal Hargarty, as McGuire was preparing to move on to the next campsite. Mulley's eyes were full of their own personal misery as he studied the gunman's injured leg. "Have to get you back to Tar City and reset it. It won't be no easy ride. There'll be considerable pain, I'm afraid."

Hooker turned his hot eyes on McGuire. "Every jolt along the way will remind me of you, McGuire—just in case I was likely to forget."

McGuire licked his dry lips. He was feeling harried and persecuted, like a rabbit scrambling from brushpile to brushpile as the dogs closed in on it.

Marshal Hargarty, for his own reasons, also had a hunted look in his eyes. He cleared his throat and looked vaguely at Willie and said, "McGuire, I arrest you for what you done back at Tar City while back. For attackin' Mr. Hooker here and bustin' his leg. I'll have to take you back and put you in the calaboose until it's settled." He glanced at Hooker and was rewarded with a grim smile of approval.

Willie looked at the marshal carefully and understood why he was doing what he was doing, but that didn't make him like it. "You're a long ways from home, Marshal. That badge of yours don't mean anything out here on the prairie."

"You done the damage in Tar City, that makes it my business."

Willie didn't know enough about the law to be sure whose business it was, he only knew that he wasn't going to go back to Tar City to be penned up like a calf fattening for the kill.

The marshal realized that taking McGuire wasn't likely to be a simple matter. Tentatively, his hand moved toward his revolver. At the same moment Pinto Gonzales stepped around the rear of the wagon, his pistol already drawn. And Matchstick, the day wrangler, rose up in the wagon bed with his own gun.

Ellie Moncrief shot pleased looks at her two wranglers, then she turned to Hargarty, smiling brilliantly. "Marshal, if anyone fires a shot my entire crew will be here in the matter of minutes. Now my wagon is ready to move on to bed-ground—I hope you're not goin' to try to stop us."

McGuire boosted Ellie Moncrief up to the driver's seat. Gonzales swung up behind the seat, grinning wearily down at the frustrated lawman. As McGuire took the lines and started the wagon on its jolting way north, he said, "You don't expect that Hooker's goin' to let things stand the way they are, do you?"

"What do you mean?" She was still pleased at having won what appeared to be an easy victory over Hargarty.

"If the gunslinger sets his mind to it, he might be able to stop your herd. He might even do it short of the Cimarron."

She scowled at him. "How could he do a thing like that?"

"Fear. There ain't many men in these parts that ain't scared of Jeremy Hooker. He says do somethin', they do it. Take that town lawman, Frank Hargarty—most likely he's decent enough, as lawmen go, when you get him off to hisself. Away from gunslingers. But you seen how he acted just now."

Ellie began to understand. "You expect there'll be other lawmen like Hargarty along the way?"

"Not only that"—McGuire waved vaguely at the brownish prairie—"there's drover supply outfits that might decide it wouldn't be too healthy to sell the Circle-M outfit what it needed. There's cow outfits that might decide not to let us cross their land. There's farmers that might try to stop the herd from gettin' at their water. Lots of things can happen—some you wouldn't believe—once a gunshark like Jeremy Hooker sets his head on somethin'."

Ellie looked at him wide-eyed. "Are you telling me that I'd be smart to let you go, because of that gunslinger?" Angrily, she shook her head. "I won't do it. I'm not scared of him."

"But maybe some of your hands are. You saw how skitterish they looked when Hooker made his threats to them."

She thought about this for a moment, and again she shook her head. "Most of the hands are regulars, they worked for the outfit when my husband was alive. They wouldn't run from Hooker and leave the herd on the prairie."

McGuire shot her a pitying look, a look that said

plainer than words that this was the kind of foolishness you had to expect when females took over the running of cattle drives. Luckily, Ellie Moncrief was looking the other way at the time.

"Besides," she said, "what would you do if I let you go? Most likely Hooker will set somebody to watching the herd—the minute you quit it he'll have another scared lawman ready to arrest you."

This time McGuire shot her a different kind of look and decided that it was just possible that she wasn't cut to the pattern of common female after all.

"Anyhow," she added, "the outfit's got to have a cook. And you're it."

"Hasn't the trail boss got anything to say about it?"

She dismissed the notion as not worth discussion. "Arnie Stone does as I tell him."

"Does that mean you'll be stayin' with the wagon?"

She gazed placidly out at the ocean of tawny grass. "*Some*body's got to get the herd to Dodge before prices fall."

five

The mistress of the Circle-M had appropriated the chuck wagon for her personal bedroom. The next morning as the last guard was riding out to the herd, Pinto found Willie bedded down on the ground and shook him awake. "You can make breakfast a little lighter this mornin', McGuire. Three hands cut their personal animals out of the remuda last night and rode. Said they'd draw their time when the outfit got to Dodge—*if* it got there."

Willie sat up and stared blearily at his partner. "Three hands quit?"

"And maybe more before the day's out. They're scared of Hooker—and I can't say I blame them."

McGuire cursed monotonously as he stamped into his boots and dampened his face at the washstand. "This herd ain't goin' to be easy to handle shorthanded." He dried his face on his shirttail and began building his first cigarette of the morning. "What we ought to do," he muttered, "is get our rigs and ride away from here. This outfit's hard luck all around."

"Harder luck out there, maybe." Pinto indicated the dark prairie. "The widow was right about one thing—Hooker ain't goin' to soon forget about

99

you bustin' his leg a second time. He's goin' to have somebody watchin'."

McGuire poured himself some of the thick brew from the coffeepot. For a time he sat on the wagon tongue, too dull and groggy to think the matter through. The longer he worried it in his mind the more hopeless it seemed. Finally he dragged himself to his feet and began hauling out his ovens and skillets, flour and lard and beef, getting ready for another breakfast.

"Once we get to Kansas," Pinto said, building up the cooking fires, "where the towns are bigger and the law a little thicker, Hooker won't have such a easy time scarin' folks into doin' what he wants."

"I've heard about Hooker until I've about had a bait of him," McGuire grumbled over his bread pan.

The sun came up burning like an iron concho just out of the forge. Willie did not take it as a good omen. And he was right.

In the first place the light crew was late getting the herd started north. Ellie Moncrief and her trail boss had a hot argument about whether or not they ought to keep McGuire on as wagon cook. Ellie was for keeping him, Arnie Stone against.

"I'm not lettin' any gunslinger like Hooker tell me how to run my outfit!"

"It's better than not havin' an outfit to run," Stone told her. "We've already lost three men, and the others're gettin' nervous. Workin' the herd is goin' to be hard enough—no sense makin' it worse by havin' a gunshark snappin' at our heels."

She stood very erect, glaring at him, her eyes flashing. "Do you think Ab Moncrief would of buckled under to the likes of Jeremy Hooker?"

"Your husband was a man, and a first-class cowman at that."

"And you figger a woman can't run the outfit, just because she's a woman."

"I never said that."

"It's what you meant. It's what you've been thinkin' ever since Ab died."

Arnie Stone's face became several shades paler. "All right, Ellie. It's your herd. I'll run it accordin' to your orders."

"My first order," she snapped, "is to get the herd movin'." Arnie wheeled and stalked angrily to his horse. "Tell the hands," Ellie called to him, "there'll be a bonus if the herd gets to Dodge before prices fall."

The trail boss mounted and rode off without replying.

Pinto had turned the remuda over to Matchstick, who had returned to the saddle in spite of his swollen ankle. He and McGuire went about breaking camp with an elaborate air of unconcern.

"Arnie hasn't got the gumption to run a trail outfit," she said, those blue eyes still flashing. "I ought to of seen that before I saddled him with the responsibility."

"He's young," Willie observed to the prairie at large. "He'll get over that."

"Maybe. But will he get over it in time to save the herd?"

"He might," McGuire said mildly. "If he gets the chance."

She wheeled and looked at Willie. "That's a queer attitude to take. I try to save your hide, and Arnie's all for throwin' you to the gunslinger— now it sounds like you're takin' his side."

Willie studied the interior of his sourdough keg and decided to add more flour and water. "Ma'am," he said slowly, "I sure don't aim to talk myself into another tussle with Jeremy Hooker. Long's you want me and Gonzales on the job, I reckon we'll stay."

After the herd had started moving, one of the hands rode back to the wagon and helped Pinto hook up the mules. That done, the rider mounted again and waited for McGuire to pull out.

"Get back to the herd," Ellie told him impatiently. "They're shorthanded and will be needin' you."

"Sorry, ma'am," the rider said politely, "but the boss man said I was to stay with the wagon."

"We don't need you. The herd does."

"Maybe so, ma'am." The hand was beginning to look unhappy. "But the boss said I was to stick with the wagon."

Ellie's tone turned cold. "I'm the owner, you take your orders from me"

"Yes, ma'am." The rider began to squirm, but he didn't rein away from the wagon.

Ellie Moncrief made an angry, unladylike sound in her throat. McGuire decided to take matters in his own hands. He hollered at the mules, cracked the lines, and the wagon lurched forward.

Around midmorning a rider appeared on a distant knoll and sat there, motionless, as the wagon jolted over the prairie. McGuire shot a nervous glance over his shoulder and was relieved to note that their escort had seen him too. The Circle-M hand was thoughtfully touching the stock of his saddle rifle. But the strange rider did not come any closer or make any threatening moves. He only sat there, watching, waiting, and no doubt mentally composing a report to Jeremy Hooker.

In Tar City a nervous Marshal Frank Hargarty was having a steadying drink in the Drover Saloon. He had had a difficult day running errands for Jeremy Hooker. It was an undignified business, but at least it was a way of staying alive. Fetch me the marshal. The liveryman. The banker. The doctor. Hooker had the whole town jumping to his whim. The townsmen didn't like it, but it had not occurred to anyone to face the gunslinger squarely and say "no." Perhaps, the marshal thought to himself, that was the reason no one had been killed.

For Hooker was as vicious as a wounded wolf. He lay in his sweltering hotel room, his newly set leg delicately supported on a down bolster. Stripped to his union suit, he lay on the sweat-soaked bed with his pistol at his side. Fetch me this man. Fetch me that man. And when he called, they jumped.

At the moment the gunslinger was conferring with the banker, Bertrand Seward. "This," the gunman told him directly, without preamble, "is what I want. One thousand dollars."

The startled banker stared at him. "One thousand dollars!" He swallowed with considerable difficulty. "A loan?"

"Naturally, a loan. Did you think I was trying to rob you? Did you think you was dealin' with a thief?"

"No, no! Nothin' like that, Mr. Hooker, I assure you!" Banker Seward was a soft round man with apple cheeks and watery eyes. "I assure you," he repeated with feeling, "such a notion never entered my head! It's just . . . it's just that a thousand dollars is such a lot of money . . ." The words trailed off in pain.

"One thousand dollars," Hooker repeated coldly.

The banker gathered himself determinedly. "May . . . may I ask what collateral you have to offer, Mr. Hooker?"

"Collateral?" The word was not familiar to him—no one had ever asked Jeremy Hooker for collateral. But he could guess what it meant. "Down at the livery barn there's my saddle and bridle." He smiled savagely. "That's your collateral, banker."

"One thousand dollars!" Seward's voice was wet with tears. "For a saddle and bridle?"

"And the word of Jeremy Hooker, banker. Do you want to tell me my word ain't worth one thousand dollars?"

Seward fumbled a blue bandanna out of his back pocket and mopped his moist brow. "Would you . . . That is, would you mind tellin' me, Mr. Hooker, why it is that you want the thousand dollars?"

The gunslinger closed his eyes. His expression was viciously dreamy. "I'm puttin' it up as a bounty on McGuire's scalp."

By midafternoon the town marshal had taken on enough liquid courage to enter the gunman's room. "Look here, Hooker, I've been overlookin' some of the things you've been sayin' and doin' here, on account of your leg. But postin' a blood bounty on a man, that's a different thing. It's murder, Hooker. I can't allow it."

Hooker showed him his steel-trap smile. "Don't fret about it, Marshal. The boys out there . . ." With a careless sweep of his hand he indicated all the outlaws who had their hideouts in nearby Indian Territory, all the renegades and sharpshooters and ridgeriders who would hear about the bounty before he could get the posters printed. "The boys out there know that Jeremy Hooker ain't a one to get somebody else to do his killin' for him. They'll grab him and hold him till I can attend to him myself. Anyway," he added casually, "long's I don't kill him inside the city limits of Tar City it's none of your affair, Marshal."

After the marshal had departed, the gunman lay for some time in savage thought. Suddenly he hollered for the hotel owner. "Has this town got a printer?"

The sweating little hotelman nodded uneasily. "There's Able Carne that gets out the county paper ever' other week. Mostly for the cattle brand advertisin'."

"Get him up here. Tell him I got a job for him."

Able Carne was a storekeeper who got out the county newspaper as a sideline. Within a matter of minutes he was standing at the foot of the gunslinger's bed, nervously mangling his hat in his sweaty hands.

"This here's what I want," Hooker told the newspaperman. "Big letters so's everybody can read it." He handed Carne a piece of ruled tablet paper on which he had written his message. The printer read it slowly to himself with moving lips: REWARD. $1,000. TO THE MAN THAT CATCHES AND HOLDS A DRIFTER BY THE NAME OF McGUIRE. LAST SEEN

WORKING AS A WAGON COOK FOR THE CIRCLE-M OUTFIT ON THE WESTERN TRAIL. THIS OFFER GOOD ONLY IF McGUIRE IS DELIVERED WITH HIS HIDE ON. SIGNED, JEREMY HOOKER. TAR CITY.

"How long will it take to get it printed?" Hooker asked.

"Not long, after I get the type set."

"Stop whatever you're doin' and get to work on it," the gunman told him. "Print up maybe a hundred posters. Take them around to the saloons. Tell the barkeeps to hand them out to everybody they see that's passin' through."

Hooker dismissed the printer by simply closing his eyes and ignoring him. For a long while he lay there without moving. A passerby glancing into the steamy room might have thought that he was asleep. Or dead. He was neither. He was dreaming—and his dream was of Willie McGuire laid out stiff and cold, with a bullet in the exact center of his forehead.

The wagon had been turned into the wind and Pinto Gonzales was dutifully digging fire trenches when the Circle-M rider appeared on the eastern horizon and came toward the wagon at the gallop. Ellie Moncrief scowled, irritated that one of her shorthanded crew would leave the herd without her permission. "It's Rusty Miller," she said. "He's supposed to be ridin' drag today."

McGuire eyed the rider uninterestedly. His mind was on his dwindling wood supply, which meant that their few sticks of firewood would have to be augmented with dry cowchips, a sorry, high-smelling fuel at best. It had been a trying day all around, what with having a woman beside him on the wagon seat all day. Not that McGuire didn't have a powerful fondness for women—it was just that his taste leaned more in the direction of dance hall girls and faro shills and drink cadgers of the trail town saloons. It was unnerving to be in the company of a "decent woman" all the time.

"Something's wrong," Ellie said, concern replacing irritation in her voice. "Look at the way he's riding."

Reluctantly, McGuire dragged his attention away from his own troubles. Ellie was right; the young drover was riding slack in the saddle, holding to the saddle horn. And there was something about his face, pale and drawn, that sent a ripple up McGuire's back. At first he thought the rider had been shot. McGuire, as wagon cook, was expected to do whatever doctoring the outfit required, and a gunshot wound was something he knew nothing about.

Risking McGuire's wrath, the hand rode right up to the wagon in a cloud of dust. Pinto hurried forward and grabbed the reins as the rider climbed weakly out of the saddle.

"Rusty," Ellie Moncrief said sharply, "are you all right? Have you been hurt?"

At seventeen, Rusty Miller was the "baby" of the outfit, alternately petted and plagued by the older drovers. "No, ma'am," he said shakily, "not hurt exactly. Just bit. Never hardly broke the hide, but . . ."

Ellie paled. "You're snakebit?"

"No ma'am." The young drover swallowed hard. "It was a mad dog."

There was an electric terror in the word. Mad dog. Most of them had seen men die from a mad dog bite. Of all the ways a cowhand knew how to die, it was generally agreed that death by rabies was the worst.

Ellie took a sharp, deep breath. Her face was almost as pale as Rusty's. She started to speak, but horror choked the words in her throat. Even Pinto was dumb for the moment, his dark eyes full of compassion as he considered this young man's terrible future.

There was also a twist in McGuire's gut as he squinted sharply at the boy's pale face. But he came forward unhurriedly and spoke in a voice so calm that it verged on boredom. "Where did he bite you, boy?"

"On the leg. I was down takin' a notch in my cinch and . . . I don't know where he came from. First thing I knowed, there he was. Right through my leggings and boots." Suddenly he held his hands behind his back to keep them from seeing how they were shaking. "Like I say, he never hardly broke the hide."

The size of the wound didn't matter. Because of a scratch no worse than a thorn prick McGuire had seen men die screaming. "Set down there against the wagon wheel," he told the boy. "Let me have a look at her."

The drover sank to the ground, his back to the wheel. With an air of brisk professionalism, McGuire unbuckled the leggings and pulled off the boot. He looked dully at the two fang marks in the lower calf. "Lucky thing you was wearin' your leggings. By the time them fangs bit through all that leather there wasn't enough poison left on them to make a groundhog sick. But we won't take no chances. I'll wash her off with coal oil and liniment, just in case."

The boy stared bleakly as McGuire swabbed the shallow wound. Not for an instant did he believe that the poison was in his leggings and not in his leg. He was as good as dead, and he knew it.

Ellie Moncrief knelt beside him; she couldn't have been more distressed if the drover had been her own younger brother. With enormous effort Rusty looked at her and made himself grin. "Don't worry about me, ma'am. McGuire's got me fixed good as new."

There was desperation in Ellie's eyes as she looked at her cook. "Is that true, McGuire?"

McGuire saw that nobody—not even Pinto—believed him. They would never believe him. When they looked at young Rusty Miller, they saw a corpse. There was no way they could keep it out of their faces. Pretty soon they would start avoiding the boy's eyes. Then they wouldn't trust themselves to look at him at all. Then, because Rusty would be convinced that he was going to die, he would die. One way or another. Like an old Comanche warrior who had convinced himself that he had outlived his usefulness, he would simply give up and die. Possibly of a bullet from his own revolver.

Suddenly McGuire lunged to his feet. "Well," he confessed freely, "of course there ain't but one *sure* way of knowin' you're safe after a mad dog bites you, and that's if you use a madstone."

All eyes turned on McGuire. Some of the misery faded from the boy's eyes. He even managed a weak smile. "McGuire, do you know somebody with a madstone?"

"I know an old Kiowa over by the Big Pasture that's got a madstone that's been in his hand longer'n anybody can recollect. The old man's daddy cut it out of the belly of a spotted deer." Willie looked at the boy and grinned brightly. "Ever'body knows that's the best kind, the ones from the belly of a spotted doe. Tell you what I'll do—I'll just get my dun and ride over there and fetch that old Indian for you."

"All the way to the Big Pasture!" There was dismay in the youth's eyes. "That'll take two days, McGuire!"

"Plenty of time," Willie said casually. "A good madstone will draw the poison out of your leg and you'll be back in the saddle before you know it."

"I wasn't thinkin' about that. The crew's already shorthanded, the herd has to keep movin'."

"The herd can keep movin'," Ellie Moncrief said. "McGuire can catch up."

McGuire turned and looked at her with an expression that bordered on respect.

"But what about McGuire?" the boy asked. "And the pals of that gunslinger that're keepin' watch on us?"

"Don't fret about me, boy," McGuire said with a confidence that he didn't feel. "I won't pull out till after dark. By the time they miss me I'll be halfway to the Territory."

Somehow—he didn't remember just how— McGuire got the outfit through supper. As darkness settled on the prairie he dug his revolver out of the chuck box and buckled it on. He was in the wagon looking for his saddle when Pinto climbed up on the front wheel and said, "McGuire, what're you up to? You don't know any old Kiowa with a madstone."

McGuire looked at him and grinned. "Maybe. But I know some Indians. And I've been told that a madstone looks pretty much like any other stone."

Gonzales stared at his partner. "You cook up this yarn about a madstone, and you ain't got the first notion where to find one?"

McGuire wrestled his saddle from beneath a pile of bedrolls. "Go catch my dun and bring him up to the wagon."

"Not till I find out what you're up to."

McGuire screwed up his homely face and thought for a moment. "There's a boy," he said slowly, "that's been mad-dog bit. He's already made up his mind he's goin' to die. Chances are a hundred to one, most likely, that none of the poison got into him. I never heard of a man dyin' of the madness when he was bit on the leg through a decent pair of boots. Them that are bit on the neck or face die ever' time; all the madstones in the Territory couldn't save them. Them with bites on their hands, maybe they got a fifty-fifty chance. Better, if they are wearin' gloves."

"Here I've knowed you all this time," Pinto said sarcastically, "and I never realized that you was a mad-dog doctor."

"I'm a looker," McGuire told him complacently, "and a watcher. And I recollect what I see."

"But you just said that them with leg bites don't die. How come you're spreadin' this yarn about a madstone and wastin' two days of the outfit's time?"

"Because that boy's got his mind set on dyin'. If somethin' ain't done he'll just lay there thinkin' about it and thinkin' about it. Then tomorrow—or the next day, maybe, when nobody's lookin'— he'll haul out his .45 and . . ." McGuire shrugged philosophically. "That's somethin' else I've seen and recollected."

"There must be some other way of changin' his mind. What's the sense of riskin' gettin' yourself shot by one of Jeremy Hooker's pals?"

McGuire shook his head. "Anything that was easy and simple, the boy would never believe. He'd know we was tryin' to put somethin' over on him."

Gonzales shook his head in wonder. "McGuire, you're loco."

"Go catch my dun. I can't set here all night jawin'."

Still shaking his head, Pinto walked off in the direction of the remuda. As McGuire climbed out of the wagon with his saddle, Ellie Moncrief pounced on him. "McGuire, do you know what you're doin'? Is there actually an old Kiowa, and does he really have a madstone?"

Frankly, Ellie Moncrief didn't know what to think about McGuire. One moment he was a common wagon cook, a moment later he was a brawler. Now, as though it were the most natural thing in the world, he had set himself the task of curing a case of rabies. "McGuire," she asked slowly, "do you really believe that a stone from a deer's belly can cure a man of a mad-dog bite?"

McGuire scratched himself and thought about it for a moment. "I've seen men that was bit get well after they had a madstone put on them. Of course, they might of got well anyhow. Sometimes it depends on what frame of mind they're in."

"And you think Rusty Miller's in a frame of mind for dyin'?"

"Yes ma'am. That's how he looks to me."

"That's how he looks to me, too." She took a deep breath and let it out slowly. "All right, McGuire. Go see if you can find a madstone."

The big dun stud had had an easy time of it in the remuda. He fought the bit and puffed out his gut when McGuire tried to cinch down. McGuire drove a knee into the animal's ribs and quickly tightened the cinch. Indignantly, the horse twisted his head and tried to bite McGuire's leg.

A few yards away Pinto sat his own animal, watching the scene with dim amusement. "I still say you're loco, chancin' gettin' yourself shot. Lookin' for an Indian that you don't even know, to get a madstone that he ain't got—that wouldn't cure a mad-dog bite anyhow, even if he did have it."

McGuire stepped into the stirrup. The dun wanted to pitch, but McGuire swung into the saddle and reined him down with no nonsense.

Gonzales asked, "Have you talked to the trail boss?"

"About what?"

"About walkin' off your job and leavin' the outfit without a cook, for one thing."

"Two days, the outfit ain't goin' to starve." He sat for a moment looking at the western ridge where they had last seen the strange horsebacker. If he was still there, McGuire could not see him.

"McGuire, you want me to go with you?"

"You got a wagon and a remuda to look after." McGuire reined the dun away from the animals of the remuda. Within a few minutes he had dissolved in darkness.

In Tar City Jeremy Hooker lay glaring up at the ceiling of his ovenlike room. For the moment he had done all that could be done. The reward money had been raised, the posters printed and distributed. The word had gone out: One thousand dollars for the whole hide of Willie McGuire.

six

His name was Print Langly. He was a nobody, thirty-three years old, saddle sore and hungry. Ever since nightfall he had been watching the Circle-M herd from a mesquite thicket. Beyond the herd he could see the cookfires and the homing lantern on the wagon tongue. From time to time he glimpsed drovers moving in silhouette against the wagon. Was that one McGuire? Or that one?

One thousand dollars! He thought for the hundredth time. It was enough to make a man's head spin. A thousand days without having to work. A thousand ways for a man to be somebody. A thousand reasons to take the small necessary chance involved in collecting the bounty.

In Tar City, Print had heard that McGuire was cooking for the trail outfit. Well, a wagon cook ought not to be so much of a problem. You simply watched and waited and played your time, and when you got your chance you threw down on him with your gun and hauled him in to Jeremy Hooker. It had seemed simple enough when he had thought up the scheme, in the Drover's bar at Tar City.

But a trail crew was a close-knit bunch, a family almost. A man had to be careful and watch for

117

just the right moment. Print had been quick to leave Tar City as soon as he had read the posters, but he had no doubt that others would be right behind him. Most likely they were out there now, some-where in the darkness. Watching, like Print. And waiting.

Well, there were times when a man had to take the bull by the horns. A thousand dollars was a thousand dollars. You couldn't sit back and wait for it to fall into your hat like spring rain.

Print set his jaw determinedly, touched spurs to his horse and moved out of the thicket.

He approached the herd cautiously. One of the men on night watch saw him almost immediately and called out, "What do you want, out there?"

Print rode in a little closer. "I smelled your coffee at the wagon and figgered I'd try to get the cook to give me some."

"Plenty of coffee, I reckon," the rider answered sourly. "Such as it is. Our regular cook ain't here, so one of the hands is doin' the dough-punchin' for a spell."

Print's mouth fell open in dismay. "The cook ain't here?"

"Went off lookin' for a madstone. One of the boys got hisself bit today."

This was disastrous news to Print Langly. "Where does he reckon to find a madstone?"

"From an old Indian, he says." The hand spat

disgustedly. "I don't put any stock in hoodoo stones, but I guess some folks do."

"Much oblige," Print said dejectedly. With a nod he reined away.

An *Indian.* Print held to that thought as he rode. It meant that McGuire was traveling east, most likely, toward the Territory. Maybe that wasn't so bad, after all. Now Print knew something that the other bounty hunters didn't know. That gave him a head start—now all he had to do was locate McGuire.

It was near midnight when Willie McGuire dismounted on the bank of some nameless creek and watered the dun. The temptation was strong to make camp here, wait a reasonable amount of time and then return to the wagon with some sort of rock in his pocket that would pass as a madstone. But he knew instinctively that it would never work. It was too easy. And nothing about a drover's life was ever easy.

If he was to make Rusty Miller believe that he was actually being cured by a madstone, then McGuire must produce not only the madstone but also the Indian that owned it. For it was well known that madstones were valuable beyond price, and a true stone and its owner were separated only by death. "Why the hell did I have to go and say an *Indian?*" Willie thought wearily. "It didn't *have* to be an Indian. It could of been anybody at all. But no, I had to say an Indian. And a Kiowa, at that!"

It was doubtful that anyone in the crew would know a Kiowa from a member of any other of the Plains tribes, but the possibility had to be considered. A mistake anywhere along the line would ruin everything. The boy, already in panic, would immediately see through a story that wasn't straight.

With a sigh, Willie lay in the damp grass and gazed up at the winking stars. To one who had not seen a man die of rabies, all his efforts might seem foolish. But McGuire, and most other cowhands, had seen it. No other death could compare with it. The worst torture of an Apache shaman was like nothing at all alongside such a death. He had known strong men to take their lives by their own hands, even before it could be proved that they had the disease. That was the kind of fear that a mad-dog bite could create. And it was the reason for the belief in madstones—for there was no other hope, once the poison was in a man's blood.

McGuire did not set himself up as an expert in the field of mad dogs and rabies, but he did know that the victim of a mad-dog bite could not be dealt with in a reasonable way. He had to be tricked. He had to be convinced that he was being cured—whether or not he actually had the disease was not always the most important thing.

Willie McGuire, who rarely thought about such

things, now casually wondered about the magic of madstones. He knew, of course, that the magic was not in the stone. It was in the desperation of a man who thought he was dying. He did not believe that a stone could cure a case of rabies—still, he had seen men who had been near death recover after the use of the stone.

Willie let his thoughts drift aimlessly. The dun grazed peacefully from the end of a stake rope. McGuire did not examine the reason for it, but there was a sense of peace that came with lying on his back and looking up at the blue-black sky. He wasn't sure just why he was going to all of this trouble because of a young cowhand that he hardly knew. It didn't matter. He had always been one to act on impulse—reason and planning had played a very small part in the shaping of his life.

The dun stud lifted its head and sniffed the night air suspiciously. McGuire didn't notice it at first. His thoughts had somehow crossed with the mental vision of Ellie Moncrief. A disturbing notion occurred to him—was the widow Moncrief somehow behind his actions? It would not be the first time that McGuire had done strange and foolish things on account of a pretty face . . .

The big stud tossed its head again and stamped the ground. This time McGuire noticed. "What is it, son? What's ailin' you?"

The dun ignored McGuire and stamped again. Nothing was ailing him. Although he had heard nothing, McGuire knew that another horse was in the vicinity. Most likely a mare.

Quickly, McGuire grabbed his .45 and rolled over on his belly. He could see nothing beyond the scrawny line of salt cedars that bordered the creek, but he knew that something—someone—was there.

McGuire mentally retraced his tracks since leaving the wagon. He realized that he hadn't been watching his backtrail—hadn't thought it necessary, although the moon was almost full and a little too bright for comfort. Perhaps it had been a mistake not to have been more careful.

Suddenly he was sure of it.

A rider materialized behind the wall of cedar. McGuire eyed the blurry figure over the barrel of his revolver. The horsebacker came forward cautiously. He had seen the dun. Already he had drawn a short rifle from his saddle boot.

"Stop right there, mister," McGuire said coldly.

The man cursed. His dark mare huffed excitedly and stamped the ground at the sight of the big dun stud. The rifle barked and a startling tongue of flame darted in McGuire's direction. The bullet ripped up the sod near Willie's elbow, snatched a neat, round hole out of his shirt sleeve and screamed into the darkness. "Hell and damnation!" McGuire bellowed in a quick rage. "The sneakin' skunk has gone and shot me!"

He jerked the trigger wildly. The rusty weapon

fired once, snapped, fired again, then jammed. Dirt or lint or possibly sourdough had worked its way into the revolver's action. No matter how hard McGuire pulled on the hammer, it wouldn't budge.

With a snarl of disgust he jammed the weapon in its holster, lunged to his feet and threw himself at the nervous mare. Luckily, the horsebacker had his hands full with the mare and was too busy at the moment to fire again with the rifle. Willie grabbed stirrup leather on the offside and clung to it grimly as the frightened animal began spinning in eccentric circles.

"Ho, goddamit!" McGuire bellowed in a fury. His feet left the ground as the mare flung him around in another circle. The animal stamped and twisted and bucked and in the process managed to twist its head around and nip McGuire's shoulder. The rider cursed and grabbed for the saddle horn and dropped his rifle.

Grabbing wildly, McGuire managed to get his big hands on the stranger's leg. With a mighty heave he tore the rider loose from his saddle, and the two of them fell sprawling to the damp sod.

Print Langly was lean and rawhide tough, but he was no match for McGuire. A huge fist loomed in his face. The night was shattered by a thousand lights. Then he felt the shock. His knees turned to water. His eyes glazed. Without a whimper he sank to the ground.

For some time McGuire sat beside his assailant, getting his breath. After a while he began crawling on his hands and knees, gathering up his own useless weapon and the stranger's short Winchester and revolver.

McGuire reached out, grabbed the rifleman by the shoulder and shook him like a coyote shaking a fieldmouse. "Might as well wake up, mister. I ain't goin' to be right happy till you do some explainin'."

Sputtering and gasping, the stranger came alive. He clawed at McGuire's big hands. "Let me go! I can't breathe!"

"I got a mind to fix it that way permanent." Coldly now, McGuire delivered another teeth-rattling shake and flung him back on the ground. "All right, now we'll talk. We'll start with who you are and what you're doin' here."

The stranger wheezed for a moment, dragging cool night air into his aching lungs. There was frank fear in his eyes as he stared up at McGuire's angry face. Somehow this was not the kind of man that was easy to picture as a wagon cook.

"Your name," Willie reminded him.

Those big hands started for him again, and the man pulled back in panic. "Langly! Print Langly!"

"Never heard of you. What's the idea tryin' to drygulch me?"

"I wasn't tryin' to drygulch you." Print Langly

gulped some more air. "I shot that one time just to scare you."

"Why?"

Print sighed. He could see that thousand-dollar bounty drifting through his fingers like river sand. Resignedly, he reached for his shirt pocket and drew out the freshly printed poster.

McGuire read it slowly in the dim light, his lips moving with every word. *One thousand dollars!* In his time McGuire had known men who could hate, but he had never known one to hate a thousand dollars' worth.

"See what it says," Print said, beginning to recover his wind and a little of his nerve. "The bounty wouldn't do me no good if I hauled you in dead. I wasn't tryin' to drygulch you."

McGuire held out the poster. "How many of these're in circulation?"

Print Langly shrugged. "Hundred or so. They're passin' them out at the Drover Saloon in Tar City." He had discarded his dream of sudden riches, but he had also lost some of his fear. McGuire, as he well knew, could be a dangerous man to play loose with—but he was no killer.

McGuire's thoughts were going in another direction. A hundred bounty hunters on the prairie, all looking for his scalp, was not a pleasant prospect.

Print grinned with sudden viciousness. "I don't know where you think you're goin', McGuire.

125

But you'll never get there. Jeremy Hooker's after your hide—and what Jeremy Hooker wants, he gets."

Willie McGuire forced himself to the painful business of thinking. Most of the bounty hunters, he reasoned, would be just starting their hunt. Most likely they'd be congregated in the vicinity of the herd, until they found out that he had pulled out. This would give him enough time to ride on to the Territory, find an Indian that was willing to cooperate, and head back. The ticklish part would come when he tried to rejoin the crew. "If I had the sense of a muley cow," he thought dejectedly, "I'd drygulch this drygulcher and strike east and make it my business never to cross Hooker's trail again."

Easier said than done. Besides, as he well knew, he could never bring himself to kill a man—even a man like Print Langly—in cold blood.

His decision made, McGuire looked at Langly and said, "Rest easy, mister, I ain't quite done with you yet." He got to his feet, went to the staked dun, got his lariat and returned. "It might just be," he said casually, "that I ain't quite a top hand with a gun. But I know plenty of things to do with a rope."

Langly's eyes widened. For a moment he wondered if he had misjudged McGuire. He was slightly relieved when McGuire knelt down and began tying his hands and feet.

"Don't fret," McGuire told him, grinning. "I aim to let you go—in a day or so. If your bounty-huntin' pals don't catch me first."

Panic was returning to Langly's bulging eyes. "Look here, McGuire, you can't leave me here to die!"

McGuire smiled and rolled him into the tall grass beneath a salt cedar. Then he caught Print's horse and stalked it in the bottom near the water. "Don't fret yourself. Long's I'm good and healthy, you got nothin' to worry about." He returned to the dun, rebitted and mounted. Langly began hollering to be let loose. He was still hollering when McGuire passed a distant rise and out of earshot.

Horses Walking, on the official records at Darlington, was a farmer. He had gone to the agency school where the Quaker missionaries had patiently drilled him in practical agriculture. They placed great stress on the practicality of farming and the folly of hunting as opposing ways of life. Finally they had furnished him with seed and the tools for turning the tough sod and cultivating the rich red earth. He was, the missionaries had assured him, prepared to participate fully in the white man's thriving economy.

Horses Walking had immediately sold the farming tools and fed the seed to his pony. Never in the history of his people had they dug in the dirt like rabbits for a living. They were hunters and warriors. They would always be hunters and warriors. No amount of missionary nonsense would change that.

However, it happened that on this particular day Horses Walking was neither hunting nor making war. He was quietly dreaming of another day, another time. He was sitting on the bank of what the white men called the Elm Fork of the Red and what the Indians called Old Woman's Creek, a cane fishing pole at his side. It was Horses Walking's carefully considered opinion that the iron fish hook was by far the white man's most important contribution to a civilized way of life, and maybe his only one.

For some time he had been watching a distant horsebacker riding slowly to the east; a big man on a big dun stallion. Now the distant rider saw him. He reined up for a moment and seemed to be turning something in his mind. Finally he kneed the dun toward the stream, fording at a rock crossing a short distance from where Horses Walking sat—scaring away all the fish as he did so. That was a white man for you.

The rider reined up beside the Indian, crossed his hands on the saddle horn and grinned. "Howdy, John. How's the fishin'?"

It was not a good beginning. Horses Walking, like all Indians, despised being called "John" or

"Chief" but the white men never seemed to notice or care. Horses Walking regarded the big rider with his dark, cool eyes.

The rider reached for the saddle rifle in the boot near his knee. Horses Walking was suddenly rigid, his eyes wide in alarm. The man, in spite of his size, did not look particularly dangerous—but it was hard to tell about white men.

Casually, the horsebacker flipped the short rifle down to the Indian. Horses Walking instinctively grabbed it out of the air. Quickly, he checked the loading and assured himself that the magazine was full. A quick flick of the lever and the rifle would be ready to fire. The face of Horses Walking became blank, but his mind was racing. Why would a white man hand an Indian a loaded rifle? What did he want? What kind of trick was this?

"It's yours," the big man told him. "If you'll do me a little favor, that is. Your fishin' ain't so important that you can't leave it for a day or so, is it?"

The rider augmented his words with enough basic Plains sign so that Horses Walking could understand him. The Indian, as a matter of pride, spoke no English.

"Is it a bargain?" the white man asked.

Horses Walking spoke no word. His blank expression did not change. Thoughtfully, he hefted the rifle in his hands. Then, with the thoroughness of a man who appreciated fine weaponry, he began to inspect the short-barreled Winchester. Obviously, it had been well cared for. It had been Print Langly's pride and joy—the stock of burled walnut, the metal blued to a satin finish. Horses Walking knew very well that he, under normal circumstances, could never afford such a rifle. His fingers caressed the cool metal with pleasure.

"Well," the horsebacker said, "how about it?"

The Indian rested the rifle across his knees, looked up at the rider and shrugged. After a moment he made the openhanded sign for question, a silent request for explanation.

The rider thought for a moment, scratching himself and sighing. "Well, she ain't right easy to put into sign, John. But a pal of mine went and got hisself bit by a mad dog. I don't think he's bad off, but he's got other notions. I figger if I can fetch him an Indian with a madstone, it might just bring him around to takin' a brighter view of the situation. He's with a trail herd over to the west of here, maybe a day's ride . . ."

Willie McGuire paused, looked carefully at those dark eyes and knew that the Indian wasn't understanding a word of what he was saying. But he understood that he was being offered the rifle in return for certain services. "One day," he said, sweeping his hand in an arc to indicate one day's travel of the sun. "You just come along and do like I say, and that rifle's yours."

Horses Walking felt his heart beating excitedly in his chest. The Winchester was a beautiful thing. More beautiful even than a good pony. He caressed the smooth wood and satin metal. Then he looked at the white man and nodded.

"It's a bargain, then," McGuire said with relief. "Just get your pony, John, and foller after me. We got us a mite of travelin' to do before the sun goes down."

The Indian pulled in his line and left his fishing pole on the bank. "By the way," McGuire said, as Horses Walking swung up to the back of his spotted pony, "I don't reckon you'd happen to be a Kiowa, would you?"

As a matter of fact, Horses Walking was Arapaho, but he had not understood the question and merely shrugged. "Well," McGuire decided, "it don't make any difference, I guess."

They made a strange pair, the big cowhand on the big stallion; the lean, brown Arapaho slouching beside him on his shaggy little pony. Horses Walking wore what was almost the Indian uniform, flop-brim cavalry hat and castoff Army shirt and trousers. He carried his new rifle lovingly in the crook of his arm, fondling it occasionally as though it were a lovely woman.

They had traveled for perhaps half an hour when they raised the small farm in the distance. McGuire pointed toward the forlorn little sod hut and said, "Pals of yours?"

Horses Walking had discovered that it was simpler to answer all questions with a shrug. He shrugged.

"You reckon they got a cow?"

The Indian looked blank.

"Milk cow," McGuire said, making milking motions with both hands.

The Arapaho shrugged again.

McGuire had suddenly remembered that, according to some authorities on madstones, the stone needed to be boiled in milk between applications. It would lend a certain authenticity to the proceedings if he could return to camp with some milk, as well as the Indian and a madstone. "Look here," McGuire told his new sidekick, "how about you ridin' over there and see if they'll let you have some milk. When we get to where we're goin' I'll give you a box of shells for that Winchester."

The Arapaho's wooden expression did not change, but his dark eyes were alive. Indeed, the rifle would be of little use without ammunition. What this big cowhand might possibly want with milk, Horses Walking could not imagine—but then, he had long since given up trying to explain the ways of the white man. Suddenly he jammed his heels in his pony's ribs and headed toward the little Indian farm at a full gallop.

Within a few minutes he came streaking back across the prairie, carrying a small syrup bucket in one hand. McGuire opened the bucket, sniffed the pale, slightly curdled liquid. It was buttermilk instead of sweetmilk, but everything considered, he doubted that anybody would notice the difference.

seven

Print Langly had managed to squirm out of the tall grass where McGuire had left him. With tremendous effort he had thrown himself over the bank of the creek, inched his way to the edge of the stream and was now impatiently soaking his bound wrists in the water.

He had hoped that a long soaking would make the hemp a bit more flexible and that he would be able to work his hands out of the rope's biting grip. But all of his work had been to no avail. His wrists were rubbed raw and the rope was as secure as it had been when McGuire had tied the knots.

The day wore on. Mild morning became blazing afternoon. Quiet panic worked its way into Print's guts. What if McGuire didn't return for him? What if he simply lay here day after day until he starved?

A short distance downstream his horse grazed peacefully. Print cursed McGuire savagely. He cursed Jeremy Hooker for tempting him with that thousand-dollar reward. He even cursed himself for his own greed. None of it did any good. He remained securely bound hand and foot.

The sun was slanting sharply to the west, the afternoon was tailing out when he heard the sound of horses. He broke into a sweat of relief. It was McGuire returning, after all. McGuire wasn't going to let him die.

"McGuire, I'm down here! By the water!"

The horses stopped for a moment and then came on at an unhurried gait. Then Print realized that there were two horses. McGuire had brought someone with him. What did it mean?

He heard the riders dismounting. Suddenly an Indian appeared on the upper bank, and Print made a little sound of alarm when he saw those cool Mongolian eyes gazing down at him. "McGuire!" he yelled. "Help me!"

Willie McGuire appeared beside the Indian, grinning down at the bounty hunter. "You been doin' more flouncin' around than a channel catfish. Well, you can stop frettin' now, we're all goin' for a little ride."

Langly recoiled instinctively. "Ride where?"

"Back to the outfit where you first seen me." Willie eased himself down the clay bank and hunkered down beside the helpless bounty hunter.

Langly eyed him uneasily. "McGuire, you're loco. The prairie between here'n Tar City's swarmin' with bounty hunters."

"I know." He whipped out his pocketknife and cut away Langly's ropes. "That's where you come in. You're goin' to see that I get back to the wagon safe and sound, bounty hunters or no bounty hunters."

Langly shook off the severed ropes and began rubbing his numb wrists and ankles. "McGuire, what're you and that redstick up to?"

"Never mind about that." McGuire grabbed him by the scruff of the neck and hauled him to his feet. He gave the bounty hunter a boost to the top of the bank. "John, you keep a watch on him. If he starts to actin' queer, shoot him through the gizzard."

During this time the Indian had not moved, had not changed his wooden expression or batted an eye. He had no notion what McGuire was up to, furthermore he did not care. He was eager only to finish the quest that McGuire had set him— whatever it might be—and return to the Territory with his new rifle.

Langly scrambled to the top of the bank, eying the Indian with apprehension. He immediately recognized the rifle that Horses Walking carried so lovingly in the crook of his arm. "McGuire," he hollered, "this redskin's got my Winchester!"

McGuire came up a cut in the bank leading the bounty hunter's roan mare. "Old John's been watchin' out after your saddle gun for you," he said placidly. "You can have it back now."

Langly stared in disbelief. "You're goin' to give me back my rifle? What're you schemin', McGuire?"

McGuire grinned. He held out his hands to the Indian and said, "Give me the rifle, John."

Horses Walking pulled back quickly, the first traces of anger showing in his dark eyes. He had got used to thinking of the rifle as his own, and he didn't mean to give it up without a struggle.

"Steady, John," McGuire said quietly, as though he were gentling a green bronc. "The rifle's yours. I gave it to you free and clear. But now I need the borry of it till we get back to the wagon."

Horses Walking understood almost none of the words; still, he sensed that this big cowhand did not mean to cheat him. He reluctantly handed over the rifle.

McGuire quickly jacked all the cartridges out of the magazine. When he was sure that the weapon was empty he handed it to Print Langly. "There you are, mister. Now get on your horse. If anybody wants to know, you're takin' me to Tar City to collect the bounty."

Langly understood what McGuire's plan was, but he was not impressed. "You don't know much about bounty hunters," he sneered. "With a thousand dollars at stake, do you figger they won't shoot me out of the saddle to get their hands on you?"

"Maybe not. Long's they don't know the rifle's empty."

Langly was beginning to look worried. "McGuire, it won't work."

"You'll think of a way to make it work," McGuire told him complacently. "Because it's the only way you've got of comin' out of this with your hide on." He drew the bounty hunter's revolver from his waistband and handed it to the Indian. "Here you are, John. If he starts actin' up, you know what to do."

Shortly before sundown the strange trio crossed the boundary of Indian Territory and entered the Texas Panhandle. McGuire rode slightly in the lead, with Langly guarding him with the empty Winchester. Horses Walking rode close to the bounty hunter, keeping a protective eye on his rifle.

Night came quietly down on the seemingly endless expanse of prairie. "McGuire," Langly repeated nervously, "this won't never work."

"It better work, or we're all good as dead."

"Even if we make it to the wagon, what good's that goin' to do me?"

"If we make it to the wagon, you're a free man, Langly. I don't care where you go from there."

Riding over the flat prairie in deep darkness gave McGuire a sense of queasiness in the pit of his stomach. He could have appreciated the anxieties of ancient mariners who feared that, if they ventured too far from shore, they might slip off the edge of the world. Though McGuire's fears were concerned mostly with the down-to-earth dangers of cut banks and dog holes, he breathed a sigh of relief when the early blackness was relieved by the appearance of a full red moon in the east. A Comanche moon. Not long ago raiding Quahada Comanches had plagued this country by the light of such moons. Now it was bounty hunters.

"Hold up a minute," Print Langly said.

They reined to a halt. For several minutes the only sound was the huffing of the horses. Then Langly pointed. "Over there. What do you see?"

On a distant rise they saw a foreign figure standing against the dark sky. After a minute the figure moved a little to one side, then seemed to back off into the night and disappear. "One of Hooker's scalp hunters?" McGuire asked.

"You can bank on it." Langly shifted uneasily in the saddle.

They nudged their animals and moved on. McGuire judged the Western Trail to be about three or four hours to the west. With a little luck they ought to make the wagon before sunup.

Then two more figures topped the rise. It looked as if their luck was running out.

"What'll we do?" Print asked worriedly.

"The wagon's where we're goin', and this is the only way to get there. I reckon we'll keep travelin' till somebody tries to stop us."

"I'd feel a heap easier if there was some shells in this rifle."

McGuire grinned. "I figger you'll think faster with the rifle empty."

Horses Walking regarded his two companions with indifference. He had not the slightest interest in their plans, his only concern was the weapon in Print Langly's hands.

Blurred shapes materialized in the darkness. "We're about to have company," McGuire said. Quickly, he drew his own battered revolver from its holster and shoved it into his waistband under his shirt. "From here on out," he told Langly, "it's up to you." He smiled widely. "Start actin' queer and John here will shoot you out of the saddle."

McGuire made out four horsebackers, spaced maybe twenty yards apart. One of them called, "Stop where you are. Set easy till we get a good look at you."

McGuire brought the dun to a halt. Langly reined up behind him, and Horses Walking stopped his pony immediately behind Langly. The four horsebackers focused on McGuire and started toward him, like a fan slowly closing. Pale moonlight shone softly on their drawn guns. One of them said excitedly, "That's the one called McGuire! I recollect seein' him in Tar City!"

McGuire could hear Langly sucking in his breath and taking hold of his nerve. "That's far enough," he told them. "McGuire's my prisoner. I'm takin' him to Hooker to get my bounty. Hard luck for you fellers, but that's the way she is."

One of the newcomers laughed unpleasantly.

"There's four of us to two of you. I reckon that changes things some." They had slowed almost to a halt; now they came forward again.

"Hold steady," Langly told them, his voice pitched a little higher than normal.

"Or you'll what?" one of the horsebackers asked with a sneer.

"Or I'll shoot McGuire right through the middle."

This surprised them. "Think about it," Langly went on coolly. "What good would a dead McGuire be to anybody? It would only make Jeremy Hooker sore, and likely as not get us all killed."

They thought about that for a minute, and they didn't like it. None of them wanted to make an enemy out of a gunslinger. They were also reluctant to let go of a thousand-dollar bounty. One of them complained, "We been out here all night, waitin' for McGuire to show his face."

"You was waitin' in the wrong place," Langly told him. "I brought him all the way from the Territory—and I aim to keep him." He jammed the muzzle of the empty rifle into McGuire's back. "Or I kill him here and now."

McGuire jumped at the feel of cold steel boring into his back. Guns—even empty ones—made him highly nervous. "Boys," he told them earnestly, "there ain't no sense losin' our heads. A thousand dollars is a lot of money. Enough for everybody, it seems like to me."

Langly smiled at the irony of McGuire's proposition. Still, he wouldn't be losing anything. Nothing divided six ways would still be nothing. On the other hand, the bounty hunters were thinking that one sixth of a thousand dollars was better than the nothing they would get if McGuire were killed. Horses Walking—the newcomers had accepted him unquestioningly as Langly's sidekick—crossed his arms on his chest and regarded the situation with profound boredom.

"I don't like it," one of the horsebackers said grudgingly, "but fair's fair. We'll all join in and haze McGuire to Tar City together."

McGuire groaned to himself. He could feel nervous sweat beading on his forehead. It was still a four-hour ride to the wagon, and the only thing keeping him alive was Langly's belief that the Indian would kill him if he did not cooperate.

The four horsebackers reined in on either side of McGuire. Lucky for McGuire, Horses Walking held his place behind Langly. They began moving west at an unhurried gait. From time to time McGuire would nudge the dun with his left knee, attempting to direct the line of march closer to the Circle-M wagon.

They had traveled for half an hour when one of the bounty hunters noticed the small syrup bucket hooked on McGuire's saddle horn. "What you got in the bucket, McGuire?"

"Buttermilk," McGuire told him.

The bounty hunter laughed. "You're real comical, McGuire. Let's wait and see how comical you are when you have to start drawin' against Jeremy Hooker."

In Tar City, Jeremy Hooker had moved from the bed to the window. With his injured leg resting on a feather bolster, he stared angrily out at the moonlit prairie. He could not bear the thought that out there somewhere McGuire was probably going about his business hale and hearty, with no pain to torment him, no fever to sear and roast him until he felt as limp and breathless as a lizard in the sun.

He closed his eyes and lay back in the chair and imagined how McGuire would look in that instant before he died. He could see the panic in McGuire's eyes, the trembling of his limbs. He could even imagine the moment of terrible fear in the man's heart.

This vision was the one thing that kept the gunman from screaming his rage. Sooner or later McGuire would be brought to him. And it would be a vision no more. It would be real.

Hooker slowly became aware of the muscles in his body, taut and quivering like fiddle strings. His breathing was labored and rapid. His teeth were on edge. The taste of steel was in his mouth.

"Easy," he told himself angrily. "It won't be long now." And after a moment he began to relax.

"Everything," he counseled himself, "comes to the man who waits." He had heard that somewhere. He didn't remember where. But it was true.

"I can wait," he said quietly to the hot, empty room. "For a little while."

He closed his eyes again. His mouth pulled to a thin, hard line across his feverish face. He was beginning to see McGuire again . . .

Well upwind from the bedded herd the Circle-M wagon stood like a silent mushroom on the moonlit prairie. Beside the front wheel young Rusty Miller lay staring up at the distant stars. Strangely, there was no pain in his leg. That, he guessed, would come later. The pain, the convulsions, the dying. It was a slow thing, he knew. There was nothing fast or easy about rabies.

If he had ever had any hope, he had given it up hours ago. The surrounding prairie was thick with bounty hunters looking for McGuire. If they hadn't already caught him, they soon would. The boy had begun to doubt that there had ever been an Indian or a madstone. He suspected that it was all a scheme of McGuire's, so that he wouldn't have to stay with the wagon and watch a man die with madness in his blood.

And the madness, the poison, was there. Rusty could feel it as it moved bit by bit, inch by inch, throughout his body. Nothing could save him, except perhaps the madstone that would not be coming. He was dying—there was not the slightest doubt of it. If I had any gumption, he thought grimly, I'd end it now, myself . . .

But the acceptance of death, at the age of seventeen, did not come easy. And besides, Ellie Moncrief had pointedly taken his revolver before throwing his bedroll beside the wagon.

In the distance he could hear the profane and tuneless singing of the night guard. He listened to the sounds that were familiar and comforting. The idle movement of the cattle, the stamping of the horses in the remuda. From time to time the night wrangler or a changing of the guard would come to the wagon for coffee. Rusty would pretend to be sleeping. He didn't want them to see how scared he was. "You all right, boy?" Rusty wouldn't budge. After a while they would ride back to their jobs.

Occasionally Ellie Moncrief, sleeping inside the wagon, would raise the wagon sheet and look down at him. Maybe, Rusty thought, to make sure that he hadn't found a gun somewhere and put an end to himself.

"I got to stop behavin' like this!" he told himself with sudden sternness. "I got to show some grit. Show them I'm not a kid like they think, but a man." Then, quite suddenly, and to his horror, tears welled up in his eyes. For some time he sobbed bitterly and silently. When the fit of self-pity was finally over he was surprised to discover that he was not quite so frightened. He even found himself thinking that maybe McGuire would come back after all, with the madstone. Hope, at the age of seventeen, did not die easily.

Pinto Gonzales, endlessly circling the remuda, was the first to see the horsebackers heading for the wagon. He immediately rode to one of the figures sleeping near the wagon. "Boss, looks like we're about to get company."

Arnie Stone was instantly awake. He threw back the tarp cover of his bedroll and began stamping into his boots. "Can you make them out?"

"Three horsebackers is all I could see. I'm pretty sure they're not from the outfit."

"Could one of them be McGuire?"

Pinto shook his head. "It ain't McGuire."

He sounded worried, and the trail boss demanded impatiently, "What is it, Gonzales?"

"I ain't sure. They're still a good piece from the wagon, and I couldn't see too much by moonlight. But, well, there's certain men that's got certain ways of ridin'. Take lawmen, they got ways all their own."

"You think we've got lawmen comin' after McGuire?"

"I don't think it's the town marshal that was here before, but it might be the county sheriff, or a deputy."

Arnie Stone stuffed his shirt into his trousers and buckled on his gunbelt. "I better talk to them. Don't want any more hands gettin' skittish and runnin' off, if we can help it."

"You want me to come with you?"

The trail boss shook his head. "No, you stay with the horses." As Pinto headed back to the remuda, Stone dropped some dry twigs on the coffee fire. The horsebackers rode into the circle of firelight. One was a big, heavy-shouldered man in his mid-forties; the other was a gangling, rawboned man who looked as if he might be an out-of-work cowhand, or a droughted-out farmer. Both men were carrying rifles in their saddle boots, and on the vest of the heavyset man was a nickel-plated badge gleaming dully in the firelight.

They rode right up to the coffee fire, closer than any wagon cook would have allowed, if the outfit had had a wagon cook on the job.

The big lawman squinted down at Stone and said, "I'm lookin' for the trail boss of this outfit. Are you him?"

Arnie nodded. "The name's Arnie Stone. The outfit's the Circle-M, makin' for Dodge. What do you want?"

The big man grinned. "I'm Hobby Walls, Deputy Sheriff of Marlin County. This here's Luke Finnel, a county posseman. We come for your cook. Bird by the name of McGuire."

Stone shoved his hat back on his head and looked up at them. "That bunch of scalp hunters out there . . ." He swept his hand at the darkness. "Are they deputies and possemen, too?"

Hobby's grin widened slightly. "Nope, they sure ain't. They're just scalp hunters, like you say. If they was to get their hands on McGuire, well, the county sheriff's office couldn't be responsible."

"What is it exactly that *you* want with him?"

"Lock him up," the deputy said placidly. "We got us a fine little rock calaboose in Tar City, so we'll just keep him there till the circuit judge comes around and tells us what to do with him."

"The judge or Jeremy Hooker?"

The lawman's good-humored grin began to fade. "That's enough jawin', Stone. I got my orders to pick up McGuire and bring him in."

"Who gave you the orders?"

"The Sheriff of Marlin County."

"I'd like to see the arrest warrant."

Deputy Hobby Walls found his grin again. He fished in his shirt pocket and produced the document, then he waited patiently while Stone read it by the light of the coffee fire. The warrant was signed by the county clerk instead of a judge, but Stone had no doubt that in Marlin County it would be considered legal.

"You're too late," the trail boss told them. "McGuire ain't here."

The lawmen sat straight in their saddles. Walls

shot an angry glance at his posseman. "Start roustin' out the hands. Tell them to get here to the wagon. The guard, the nighthawk, everybody."

A quiet, angry voice spoke up immediately. "Sit where you are—unless you're just achin' to get shot."

Ellie Moncrief, in a white cotton wrapper, rose up behind the wagon seat, grasping a cocked .45 in both hands. Where she had found the revolver, Arnie Stone didn't know. Probably she had taken it from the warbag of one of the sleeping hands. He turned to look at her, speaking with the voice of a man whose patience was being sorely tried. "Ellie, let me handle this."

"I can see how you was about to handle it, and I don't like it." Her eyes glinted angrily. "I'm tired of talk. I'm tired of havin' my outfit plagued with bounty hunters. Tell them to turn around and ride away from my wagon before I decide to shoot them both."

The sight of this ghostlike woman with the trembling .45 in her hands clearly disturbed the two lawmen. The deputy looked about uneasily and cleared his throat. "Ma'am, I got a warrant, legal and proper, to arrest your wagon cook."

"My cook ain't here. And if he was, I wouldn't let you have him. Now are you leavin', or do I have to start shootin'?"

The lawmen were beginning to sweat. At one end of the string Jeremy Hooker waited for them to bring in Willie McGuire, at the other end was an angry woman with a cocked .45 in her hands. Taken all in all, Hobby decided he'd rather face the gunslinger.

The lawmen began to back their animals away from the circle of firelight. "The sheriff ain't goin' to like this. He's goin' to be right put out when I come back to town without McGuire!"

"Git!" Ellie snapped angrily, her finger tightening on the trigger.

The two lawmen got.

As Ellie lowered the .45 there was the light of triumph in her eyes. She was proud of herself for meeting the situation head-on and winning. "Arnie." The word crackled with impatience. "Arnie, when are you ever goin' to get the gumption to deal with no-accounts like that? Sometimes I wonder why I ever hired you as trail boss."

The trail boss closed his eyes for a moment. He seemed to be grinding his teeth. "If you had started a shootin', Ellie, most likely we wouldn't of had any herd left. All the years you've been around cattle, don't you know how little it takes to start a stampede?"

Clearly, the possibility of a stampede had not occurred to her. The thought of it now caused her to pale. Cattle running wildly to the four winds. The lives of good horses and men placed in jeopardy. The very best that could come out of a stampede was the loss of hundreds of pounds of beef weight. Had her hardheadedness almost caused such a thing to happen?

For a moment the thought dismayed her. But in the end she determinedly pushed it away. It was only further proof of her trail boss's lack of gumption. "Arnie," she told him coolly, "go back to sleep, the trouble's over. Let me know," she added, "the minute McGuire gets back."

McGuire and his six-man escort had been riding for two hours when three more bounty hunters bore down on them from a dark thicket of mesquite. "Hard luck, boys," Willie told them cheerfully. "These here fellers beat you to me."

The latecomers didn't like it, but there was little they could do. They were outnumbered six to three—or seemed to be. During the brief, angry exchange Horses Walking never moved from his position directly behind Print Langly, his dark eyes never left the gleaming beauty of his rifle.

"Better luck next time," McGuire called, as the three scalp hunters headed reluctantly back to Tar City.

A few minutes later they were stopped by a pair of out-of-work cowhands, both of them with Jeremy Hooker's reward posters in their pockets. Several times they were stopped by groups of twos or threes, most of them amateurs at the art of scalp-hunting and easily turned back with a show of force.

Then the inevitable happened. On a distant knoll McGuire glimpsed the large cluster of horsemen. More than a dozen of the hard-luck adventurers had banded together, their apparent aim being to take McGuire away from his captors. "Boys," McGuire told them truthfully, "I don't much like the looks of this."

One of the riders hollered, "We come to get the wagon cook. We aim to take him, easy or hard. It's up to you!"

McGuire felt a cold sweat forming on the back of his neck. The band of bounty hunters began closing in on them. Print Langly was also looking worried. McGuire glanced at him and moved his head slightly to the left. Langly nodded.

A voice from the pack called, "There ain't no use holdin' back, boys. We got the deputy sheriff with us and we got us a warrant."

McGuire turned to look at his escort. "Gents," he said gravely, "I'm goin' to tell you the truth. I never had a heap of luck with deputy sheriffs. If somebody has to collect the bounty, I'd rather it was you than him. Way I see it, only chance we got is to split up in two or three bunches. By the time they figger out which bunch I'm with, we can get ourselves lost in the brush."

The four latecomers looked blankly at one another. They could only see that their share of the bounty was about to be snatched away from them by the larger pack; they were tempted to grab at any chance that might save it for them.

But one of them was suspicious about letting the prisoner out of his sight. "Who's goin' to stay with McGuire? And how do we know the rest of us will get our fair piece of the bounty?"

"What's to fret about?" McGuire asked impatiently. He was thinking with unusual clarity now; his life depended on it. "Whoever's with me has to take me to Hooker to collect the money. The rest of you can meet up at Tar City."

The late arrivals were far from satisfied with this solution, but the rival pack was closing ground fast. Sweat glistened on their faces. Still they hesitated.

McGuire decided to take things into his own hands. With another warning glance at Print Langly, he suddenly kicked the big dun's ribs. As McGuire spurted across the dark prairie, Langly hesitated only an instant. Horses Walking was close behind him, watching him intently. With what appeared to be a sigh of resignation, Langly also spurred his animal after McGuire, and Horses Walking followed less than half a length behind.

For a few moments the new arrivals were thrown into confusion. The remainder of McGuire's escort split in two and spurred away in opposite directions. The deputy's pack began to mill and holler. Someone, in his frustration, began firing blindly.

For the moment McGuire and Langly and Horses Walking were all alone. They raced at breakneck speed across the dark plain. They were only too aware of the dangers of dog holes and cut banks, but McGuire was running for his life. Print Langly was running because he still believed the Indian would kill him if he didn't. Horses Walking was running because he refused to let his cherished Winchester out of his sight.

McGuire crashed into a thicket of mesquite, the thorny limbs almost snatching him out of the saddle. Langly and the Arapaho charged in behind him, like three bullets out of the same rifle. They bulled through the thicket, raced headlong down a rocky grade, then streaked northwest along what appeared to be a deer trail.

The big dun, feeling the pace, was beginning to grunt its resentment. Langly's mount was weaving dangerously. Only Horses Walking's little spotted pony seemed as strong as it had been when the reckless race had started.

At last they came to a growth of brush beside a dry wash and McGuire stopped to let the dun blow. He studied the prairie intently. It stood still and peaceful in the moonlight. He began to grin. "Boys," he said happily, "it looks like we made it."

They came to a stream that McGuire remembered from the day before. "Gents, if I ain't mistook, the Circle-M wagon ain't more'n an hour from here."

The sustained fear that came from riding hell bent across a dark prairie had left Print Langly limp. "McGuire," he said sincerely, "I hope you rot in hell for this."

Willie McGuire laughed. He was feeling in top shape now. He had traveled all the way to the Territory and back without getting caught. He had his Indian and his buttermilk . . .

Suddenly he slapped his forehead with the flat of his hand and groaned. "Hell and damnation! I clean forgot what it was that I left camp for!"

He dumped out of the saddle and began digging in the gravelly soil beside the stream. Quickly, he collected a double handful of small rocks and began inspecting them in the moonlight. One he discarded as too small. Another was too large. Some were sharp-edged, others were too smooth. He let them drop to the ground. Once he looked up at Horses Walking and said, "John, if you was the actual owner of a madstone, what do you reckon it would look like?"

Horses Walking looked at him and shrugged. All white men, he had found, were somewhat addled—this one was just a bit more so.

At last McGuire grunted with satisfaction. The stone he had settled on was about the size of a four-bit piece, whitish in color and porous in texture. He handed it up to the Arapaho. "Hold onto this, John. I'll get it back from you when we get to the wagon."

The Indian took it unquestioningly and dropped it into the pocket of his shirt. McGuire slapped his hands together. "Gents, the quicker we get to the wagon, the quicker we'll have the business settled."

Print Langly, with the air of a man who knew that he was about to make a fool of himself, said, "McGuire, what do you aim to do with a bucket of buttermilk and a rock?"

"Cure a mad-dog bite," McGuire answered, as he climbed back into the saddle.

Langly did not look surprised. It was about the kind of answer he had expected.

eight

Pinto Gonzales was restlessly circling the remuda when the three riders rode out of the darkness. He recognized the big dun and the big rider immediately. It did not seem possible that a man in his right mind might regret the loss of the dangerous companionship of Willie McGuire, but such was the case with Gonzales. Since early morning he had been aware of the bounty hunters swarming in the darkness. For the best part of an hour he had given McGuire up for lost. It seemed highly unlikely that he could make his way back through that pack of money-hungry wolves.

There was no denying that Pinto was glad and relieved to see his sidekick again, but he sternly resisted any temptation to show it. Instead, with forced calm he built himself a smoke and lit it, and barely allowed himself to notice the trio as they headed toward the remuda.

"I guess you know," he reminded McGuire, when they closed to speaking distance, "that the outfit's been held up on account of you. The boss'll be sore's a saddle gall if you don't get breakfast ready on time."

McGuire grinned. "I guess." Suddenly he reached around and took the rifle from the man who was following him and handed it to the

Indian. "Light out, Langly. If you're lucky you can make it out of the county a jump ahead of that deputy's posse."

Langly glowered angrily. "Like I said before, McGuire, I hope you rot in hell for this."

McGuire waved his hand wearily. "Git."

The would-be bounty hunter reined away from the remuda. He hesitated for a moment, trying to think of a parting shot that would be appropriate to the occasion, but in the end he wheeled angrily and rode back into the blackness of the early morning.

Pinto said dryly, "I don't guess it would be any use askin' what's goin' on here?"

"Later," McGuire told him. "How's the boy?"

The nighthawk spread his hands and shrugged. "Sick. From the way he looks, I think maybe the poison's already in his blood."

McGuire snorted and motioned to the Indian. "Foller me, John. We'll go take a look at the patient."

The camp was already beginning to stir. Ellie Moncrief, the substitute cook, and the day wrangler were all struggling with the ovens and skillets when McGuire and Horses Walking tramped into the circle of firelight. Ellie stared at McGuire for almost a full minute before she realized that her hands were full of pounded steaks ready for frying. With only a brief glance at the Indian, she began dropping the steaks into sizzling fat. "I sent Arnie and some of the boys to look for you, hopin' maybe they could work you back through that pack of scalp hunters. Did you see them?"

McGuire shook his head and poured himself some coffee. "Nope. How's the patient?"

"He looks bad to me." She sounded as if she hadn't slept since McGuire had left camp. "I don't think he wants to live anymore."

McGuire gulped his scalding coffee. "I brought old John here, with this madstone. He'll fix the boy up good as new." He motioned for the Indian to follow him, and they moved to where the still figure lay beside the wagon wheel. "How do you feel, boy?"

Rusty Miller looked up at McGuire with terror-filled eyes. ". . . All right, I guess."

"Leg givin' you any trouble?"

The youth forced a trembling smile. "It's too early for that, most likely."

"I guess." Suddenly McGuire beamed. He clapped his big hands together, and his voice boomed with the brash confidence of an Irish track-walker. "Well, now! You got nothin' to fret about, boy. I went over to the Territory and brought old John back, just like I said I would." He grabbed Horses Walking by the shoulder and pulled him into the light. "John, show the boy the reason I hauled you in all the way from the Territory. Show him the madstone."

Horses Walking was beginning to look dubious about the whole affair. He cocked his head and eyed the big cowhand speculatively with his dark eyes.

"The stone," McGuire was saying impatiently. "The madstone. Let the boy see it." He shot a grin at Rusty Miller. "You got to keep in mind, boy, that old John's a full-blooded Kiowa. Don't talk our kind of talk. On top of that, of course, a first-class madstone's a powerful valuable thing. Makes John a big man amongst the Kiowas. Well, I guess you can just figger how much trouble he has, holdin' onto a valuable thing like that. Hardcases tryin' to rob him. Sharpshooters tryin' to beat him out of it. Makes him sorta skitterish about showin' it around sometimes." Suddenly raising his voice, he wheeled and hollered at the Arapaho, "Hell's afire, John, show the boy the madstone!"

As though by sheer volume McGuire had made himself understood, Horses Walking reached cautiously into his pocket and drew out the small rock. "There she is!" McGuire said proudly, holding it out for the young drover to see. "Never been known to fail!" Well, McGuire thought to himself, *that* much is true, anyway. "Old John's pa found it hisself, right in the belly of a spotted doe. Most famous madstone in the whole damn Territory!"

The youth stared at the stone with burning eyes.

He couldn't believe it. He was afraid to allow himself to believe that the stone was real. "McGuire, you wouldn't lie to me, would you?"

"Lie to you!" McGuire bellowed in outrage. He glared indignantly around at nearly a dozen faces glowing red in the firelight, without realizing that Arnie Stone's party had returned to the wagon, or that he had raised the entire camp with his bellowing. "*Lie* to you!" He hollered again. "Boy, is that the kind of thanks I get for all the troubles and miseries I went through on account of you? Boy, that hurts me." He pounded his chest with his fist to show where the pain was.

Rusty Miller looked vaguely stunned by all this uproar. Some of the drovers grinned uncertainly. Arnie Stone pushed through the circle of faces. "How'd you get through that pack of scalp hunters?" he demanded suspiciously.

"That," McGuire said with feeling, "is a long story."

"Where did this Indian come from?"

"This Indian," McGuire said, clapping his hand on the Arapaho's shoulder, "just happens to be the head witch man of the Kiowas. Me and him are pals from the days when I used to scout for the cavalry."

The trail boss blinked. He was on the verge of sneering. "I never heard that you was a cavalry scout."

"Lots of things," McGuire told him, "that you

ain't heard about." But the truth was, he had never been within shooting distance of a cavalry outfit and he didn't know what had caused him to say it. He was considerably relieved when Ellie Moncrief grabbed her trail boss by the sleeve and said, "McGuire has gone to a lot of trouble tryin' to help Rusty. Maybe he even risked his life."

Stone allowed himself to be pulled back into the circle of drovers. "All right," he said grudgingly, "you brought back an Indian. And a stone—of some kind." Clearly, he was not impressed with either. "Now let's see how good you are at curin' mad-dog bites."

"Just what I aimed to do," McGuire told them in what he supposed was a tone of quiet dignity. "You," he said, pointing to the day wrangler, "fetch me an airtight."

The startled wrangler rustled in the wagon supplies and returned with an empty tomato can. McGuire inspected it minutely and returned it. "Rinch it out."

The puzzled wrangler went to the water barrel and carefully rinsed the tin can. This time everything seemed to be to McGuire's satisfaction. The circle of drovers watched their cook's every move as he carefully pried the lid off the syrup bucket and poured a little of the buttermilk into the can. "Put this on the fire and keep it hot."

One of the drovers took the can and placed it on the iron spider beside the coffee. McGuire held the "madstone" in his left hand—the eyes of the entire crew were fixed on it. He rested his right hand on the wagon wheel, dipped a bit of axle grease on his index finger and held it there out of sight. Then he knelt beside the stricken cowhand. "You ever see a madstone, boy?"

Rusty Miller shook his head. McGuire held the stone out at a safe distance and the youth stared at it in fascination.

"She don't look like so much," McGuire admitted. "Almost like a common rock, you might say. But it ain't the way she looks that's important. It's the way she works—ain't that right?"

Hardly daring to hope, the young cowhand nodded. The standing drovers found themselves nodding with him. With abrupt briskness, McGuire said, "All right, boy, it's time we got down to work." With an air of unquestionable professionalism, he unwrapped the bandage on the boy's leg and inspected the tiny wound. With heavy authority, he looked up at the circle of faces and told them, "First thing's got to be done is scrape off some of the hide. Give the madstone a fair chance of drawin' the poison."

Heads nodded involuntarily. Slightly glazed eyes stared as McGuire drew out his knife and energetically scratched the skin that surrounded the wound. Nothing good ever came easy. This was a principle that every cowhand believed in. The more bitter the medicine, the quicker the cure.

The young drover winced, but McGuire continued scratching until the area was raw. Then, with a flourish, McGuire slapped the grayish stone to the raw patch of flesh and held it in place with a turn of the bandage.

"Feel anything yet?"

The bug-eyed youth shook his head abstractedly. "I ain't sure."

"Might take a little while," McGuire told him. He sat back on the ground, built himself a cigarette and smoked it leisurely. The crowd of standing drovers seemed to be holding its breath. Only McGuire seemed unconcerned—and the stone-faced Arapaho, standing with his arms folded across his chest, looking profoundly bored by it all.

"Bring the milk," McGuire said at last, and the wrangler scurried to the fire and brought back the tomato can half full of hot buttermilk. Well aware that his every movement was being watched, McGuire, with the instincts of a professional stage actor, unwrapped the bandage and removed the stone. "Now," he said, falling into the extravagant style of a traveling lecturer, "we'll see if she's started to draw out the poison."

He dropped the stone into the can, and as he did so he managed to dip the finger with the axle grease into the hot milk. "Now," he said to the wrangler, "give 'er a good boilin'."

The can was returned to the fire and the

buttermilk was boiled at a lively rate for several minutes. "I reckon that ought to be enough," McGuire said finally. "Let's have a look at her."

The curious drovers ganged around the coffee fire as McGuire tilted the can, allowing the firelight to dance on the murky green mixture of axle grease and milk. There was a hissing sound, breaths were released. Somebody asked huskily, "Is that the poison that come out of the stone, McGuire?"

"Course, it's the poison. Look at that milk. Ugly as skunk bile, ain't it?" He cleared a path through the drovers and showed the poisonous-looking milk to Rusty Miller. "I told you that was a first-class madstone, boy. She's already started to draw. I wouldn't be surprised if you wasn't up and in the saddle again before dinnertime."

The boy stared at the sickish liquid in the can. There could be no doubt that anything so ugly had to be poison. The poison had come from the stone, the stone had come from the place on his leg where the mad dog had bitten him. The pieces fell together and made a beautiful, irrefutable logic in the young cowhand's mind. "It's really the poison, McGuire! I can see it with my own eyes!" The color of life began to appear in his dead-white face. "McGuire, it's workin'!"

"Course it's workin'. Like I told you." McGuire prepared to dash the hot milk onto the ground when Ellie Moncrief stepped in quickly and grabbed his hand.

"I want to see that, McGuire." There was a strange glint in her eyes. The corners of her mouth were pulled down grimly. After studying the contents of the can for several seconds she handed it back to McGuire and asked coolly, "Is that all there is to it?"

"Yes, ma'am," McGuire told her. "Far as it goes. Course, the madstone can't draw out all the poison all at once. We'll have to keep puttin' it on and boilin' it till the poison stops showin' in the milk."

"How long will that take?"

McGuire shrugged. He didn't like the look in those cool blue eyes. "Can't tell exactly. Depends on how much poison he's got in him, I reckon."

She looked at him quietly for what seemed like a long time. At last she nodded. "All right. Go on with your doctorin'. The rest of you start gettin' the herd ready to move. Breakfast in half an hour."

The crew moved reluctantly. In their faces was the look of men who had just witnessed a miracle. In their minds they had written the young drover off as dead, but now it appeared that McGuire was giving him new life. A wagon cook with the gift of life in his hands. It was a thought that staggered their imaginations.

Pinto Gonzales brought up the saddle band and turned it over to the day wrangler. He and Ellie

Moncrief hurriedly set the sourdoughs on to bake and began frying the half-pounded steaks. McGuire, finding himself in an unusually privileged position, continued to apply the stone to the youth's leg, boiling it thoroughly in buttermilk after each application. Each time he boiled the stone, the milk became a little lighter. And each time more color appeared in the boy's face. The light of life was in his eyes. He smiled. "McGuire, it's workin'! It's really workin'!"

"Hell's afire, boy, you don't reckon Willie McGuire would ride clean to the Territory just to rustle up a hoodoo stone that wouldn't work, do you?"

The first bunch of drovers rode in from the herd and ate their breakfast in awed silence. Rusty Miller, the boy who had been the picture of death a few hours before, now sat upright against the wagon wheel. "Look at that, boys! There ain't hardly any poison in the milk at all!"

Sure enough, when Willie fished out the hot stone and dumped the milk to the ground it was barely tinted with green. McGuire also noted that the bead of axle grease on his finger was almost gone.

The crew finished breakfast without complaint, although the steaks were tough and stringy, the biscuits burned on the bottoms and raw in the middle. The gravy that Ellie Moncrief had distractedly mixed in one of the skillets would, as the saying went, turn the point of a skinning knife.

When the crew had returned to the herd, Ellie put Pinto to breaking camp. "McGuire," she called, her voice flinty, "I want to talk to you."

"In a minute," McGuire was leisurely binding the stone to the young drover's leg for what he hoped would be the last time.

"Now!" she turned and snapped at him.

Puzzled, Willie left his patient and walked with her a good distance from the wagon. "Now!" she said suddenly, her voice fairly hissing in agitation. "What's all this damn foolishness about, McGuire? I seen you smearin' dabs of axle grease inside that can to give the milk a bilious tinge. Who was you expectin' to fool with a trick like that?"

Slightly bug-eyed, McGuire stared at her. "Fact of the matter is, ma'am," he said ponderously, "I was hopin' to fool the boy. It's a good thing for him that he ain't got your suspicious nature."

Her eyes flashed. "Look here, McGuire! You've been wastin' the outfit's time. You did bring back an Indian, but he's a long way from bein' a Kiowa, as any cowman that has ever sold beef to the reservation would know in a minute. You brought back a 'madstone' that is a common gray rock like anybody can pick up on the prairie. Lord knows where you got the buttermilk, or why. I never heard of buttermilk bein' used in the treatment of mad-dog bites, and I don't think anybody else

170

ever did. You've been trickin' that boy right along, with everything you did. I want to know why."

"If you'd leave off talkin' for a minute," Willie told her wearily, "I'll be proud to tell you."

She pulled up short, glaring at him. "You're right," McGuire told her mildly. "Old John's just an Indian, and most likely not a Kiowa at all. The madstone's just a rock, like you say. The prairie's covered with them. The buttermilk—well, it was just for show. Somethin' I happened to think of when I was headed back from the Territory. Put them all together and I don't reckon they'd cure a mosquito bite."

Ellie stared up at that homely face. She fairly quivered in her indignation. "Trickery! Everything you did was trickery!"

"Yes ma'am," McGuire admitted. "I guess that's what it was. But maybe you recollect what I said just before I left for the Territory. Sometimes a man—a man like that kid drover of yours—gets it in his mind that he's goin' to die. And that's what he'll do, if somethin' don't change his mind for him. That's where I figger the madstone comes in. If it's doin' any good it ain't in his leg, it's in his head."

Suddenly that moment came back to her, and it disturbed her. She remembered the death-gray mask that had already settled on Rusty Miller's face. Everybody, including Rusty, had been convinced that the poison of madness was in his blood. Everybody but McGuire. Now she turned and looked at the young drover and saw him glowing with life.

The anger went out of her. She sighed. "Go ahead. Do whatever you think is necessary."

Around midmorning Horses Walking shoved Print Langly's revolver into his waistband, cradled his Winchester lovingly in the crook of his arm and rode back to the Territory. His brief and mysterious association with the big cowhand called McGuire had left him more convinced than ever that the way of the white man was indeed strange.

Early that afternoon Jeremy Hooker received the news that Willie McGuire had slipped through the fingers of his personal scalp hunters. He did not receive it kindly. For some time he sat glaring out of his hotel room window at the seething prairie. He realized only too well that the situation was rapidly getting out of hand. Folks were beginning to say that a common wagon cook was making a fool out of Jeremy Hooker. They were beginning to think that maybe the gunslinger was losing his grip.

Nobody had to tell Hooker that a thing like this, for a gunslinger, could be fatal. Brassy young toughs with reputations yet to make would begin to wonder if the Hooker draw had slowed. If his aim had become less deadly. And some of them would find it necessary to test it for themselves. Always a dangerous business.

Luck had a way of weighing the chances on the side of the young, as Hooker knew very well. A sudden shift of wind, a bit of dust in your eyes, a blink at the wrong time, and you were dead. Even if your name was Jeremy Hooker.

There had been a time when he might have passed the situation off with a shrug, without serious loss of face. If he hadn't been in such a rage, if he hadn't pressed so hard, McGuire would have lit out for distant places, and that would have been the end of it. A broken leg was not comfortable, but neither was it a mark of shame. It was one of those things that happen in trail town saloons, and it might have happened to anybody. But Hooker hadn't let it rest. He had made such an issue of it that now the whole country knew about it. All the way from the Bravo to the Platt, wherever men gathered around campfires, there would be talk of the wagon cook that had broken Jeremy Hooker's leg.

There was no backing away from it now. No pretending that it might have happened to anybody—it had happened to Jeremy Hooker. That made the difference.

He summoned Frank Hargarty, and in a matter of minutes the quaking town marshal was in the room. "How many drover supply outfits in this town, Hargarty?"

The question seemed to surprise and worry the marshal. "One main one, the Trail Supply Company. Course, other places do business with trail outfits. Harness maker, feed dealer, blacksmith."

The gunman's eyes became glittering slits. "Tell them they're not to do business with Circle-M until they turn loose of McGuire. No supplies sold, no harness mended, no horses shod. Nothing."

The nervous marshal took a bandanna and mopped his face. "I'll tell them, but they won't like it."

"Tell them it's what Jeremy Hooker wants. They don't have to like it."

When the marshal was out of the room, the gunman sent for the deputy county lawman, Hobby Walls. The deputy sheriff was not the rabbit that the marshal was, but neither did he intend to make an enemy of a famous gunslinger. "How much longer do you figger the Circle-M herd will be in your county, Deputy?"

Walls shrugged. "Two days, maybe, allowin' ten to twelve miles a day."

Once more the gunman's eyes became shining slits. "That gives you two days to bring McGuire to me."

The deputy started to bristle, but he quickly

remembered who he was talking to and kept his tone respectful. "That won't be easy. Trail outfits hang together. It would mean a fight."

"Let them fight. They've got a herd to look after, that's the important thing with cow outfits. Put a few shots into the leaders—maybe a little stampede will change their minds for them."

The lawman paled. "I don't think the sheriff would like that. I don't think anybody would. It would give the county a bad name with other outfits comin' up the trail. First thing you know they'd start bearin' away from Tar City—and that would mean the end of this town."

For a time the gunman said nothing, but there was murder in his face. "I leave it to you, Deputy. I don't care how you do it. But get me McGuire."

McGuire was almost happy to get back to his ovens and skillets. While hovering over a Dutch oven to see that his sourdoughs were browning properly, the threat of Jeremy Hooker seemed a long way off.

And there was something else—a faintly mystifying air about the outfit—that puzzled McGuire at first, and then pulled him up with pride. "Them sourdoughs wasn't too bad this mornin', McGuire." Rare praise, from an over-worked drover to a wagon cook. "McGuire, you got a good scald on the gravy this time. It was almost fit to eat." Two compliments in one morning—it was unheard-of adulation!

"Before your hat begins to shrink," Pinto Gonzales told his sidekick, "it ain't the grub they're really talkin' about, it's the kid."

Rusty Miller, who, not many hours before, had grimly braced himself for death, had saddled that morning with the rest of the crew and was now back to riding drag. McGuire understood that it was possible to speak lightly of gravy and sourdough biscuits; with death it was not. By complimenting his cooking they were silently thanking him for what he had done for the young drover.

Also there had been a quiet and subtle change in Ellie Moncrief. Several times that morning McGuire had looked up suddenly and had seen her standing there beside the wagon, watching him intently, with a thoughtful shine in her eyes. Once she colored slightly and said, "McGuire, that was a fine thing you did for Rusty. The crew appreciates it. I appreciate it."

Now, being appreciated was a fine thing, and Willie McGuire had often thought to himself that he had not had his share of it. But at that moment he found it somehow disconcerting. He scratched himself for a considerable time and finally said, "Ma'am, I'm right proud the boy's back in the saddle again, but if it's all the same to you, I'd just as soon let it drop."

She smiled—and even the smile was not the same. Willie groped for a word to describe it and was vaguely disturbed to find that the word was "feminine." Suddenly it was hard to believe that this was the determined, hardheaded female who a short time before had held an unwavering .45 on a deputy sheriff.

Later that morning, as they were breaking camp, McGuire turned to Pinto Gonzales and demanded, "Does it seem like to you that the widow is beginnin' to turn a little queer?"

Pinto grinned toothily. "I noticed. So has the boss, Arnie Stone."

McGuire scowled. Now that he thought about it, it did seem like Stone had treated him with considerable coolness that morning, while the rest of the hands were going out of their way to be pleasant. "What do you make out of it?"

"Looks plain enough to me. The widow's stuck on you, McGuire."

McGuire looked blank for several seconds. Then his face began to glow. "You're loco! Gamblin' hall gals up at Ellsworth is more *my* style!"

"I never said it made sense," Pinto smirked. "I'm just sayin' how it looks."

"Loco!" Willie rattled pots and skillets furiously.

nine

The first shot came out of a thornbush thicket, less than two hundred yards from the point of the herd. A steer stumbled and dropped in its tracks.

For one electric moment the herd was poised to run. The scout, Shorty Eller, took his life in his hands and plunged into the leaders. As he turned the point to the east, the swing riders raced forward and dragged the fallen beef away before the smell of blood could stir the excited cattle to stampede. Arnie Stone and one of the other swing riders drove iron to their mounts and spurted toward the rifleman.

They were too late. The bushwhacker had pulled back into a deep arroyo. A fight here could tie up the whole crew. The entire herd could be lost.

After the crew had turned the herd and begun to gentle the nervous animals, Eller scouted the area directly ahead. After a few minutes he returned with a white paper in his hand.

"I found this pegged to the ground, with a pile of rocks behind it." He handed the find to Arnie Stone.

The paper was one of Jeremy Hooker's reward posters. On the back was a brief message written with the lead end of a bullet. *"This is your last warning. Turn over McGuire."*

The trail boss studied the message with a grim face. "I'm goin' to the wagon," he told the scout. "Keep the herd movin'."

McGuire was laying out his ovens for the mid-day meal when he saw the trail boss streaking in from the herd. At the last minute Stone reined around to the lee of the wagon and dismounted.

Ellie Moncrief, who had been helping McGuire with the sourdoughs, looked up and scowled. "Arnie, do you have to fog up so much dust when you ride into camp?"

"There's worse things than grit in the biscuits," the trail boss told her. He handed her the message left by the bounty hunters. Then he told her about the shot that had been fired into the point of the herd. "If it hadn't been for Shorty Eller there'd be Circle-M cattle all over the Panhandle and some of the Territory by this time. And like they say, that was just a warnin'. They're holdin' the high card, Ellie. We've got to do like they want."

Ellie's mouth turned down. Her eyes were cold. "No."

McGuire, with a sure instinct for survival, guessed unhappily at what they were saying. He put aside his pots and pans and tramped over and read the message over Ellie's shoulder. "One thing you got to give that gunslinger," he said ruefully, "he's determined. Well . . ." He shrugged elaborately and began to take off his apron.

"What do you think you're doin'?" Ellie snapped.

"Ma'am," McGuire told her carefully, "I'm much obliged for the work you gave me and Gonzales, but now it's time we lit out."

She snorted. "With that pack of scalp hunters waitin' for you? You wouldn't last out the mornin'."

A yellow-haired swing rider by the name of Cornsilk topped a rise to the east of the herd and loped toward the wagon. He reined up a respectable distance from the cooking fires and got down. "Boss," he said to Arnie Stone, "we've got the cattle quieted down and pointed north again. Shorty Eller says we ought to be out of the county before sundown, with a little luck."

Ellie smiled. "Much oblige, Cornsilk. How does the rest of the crew feel about this?"

The hand blinked. "About what, ma'am?"

"About stickin' with the outfit. There's been some talk . . ." She shot a meaningful glance at Arnie Stone. "There's been some talk that the hands was startin' to get skitterish."

The rider helped himself to coffee and looked thoughtful. "Well," he said slowly, "it's a fact that the boys ain't in no big hurry to see the cattle start runnin'. On the other hand, like Shorty says, we'll be out of the county by sundown. There'll be a new set of county lawmen to deal with, and maybe they won't be so quick to let Jeremy Hooker run their business for them."

"The boys are willin' to stick with the outfit, then? In spite of the danger?"

"Yes, ma'am. I reckon we owe that much to McGuire, for what he done for Rusty." He finished his coffee and grinned self-consciously. "Anyhow, McGuire's the only cook we got, and I reckon we've got to eat."

Ellie turned to her trail boss in cool triumph. "The hands are willin' to take their chances. You seem to be the only one that wants to hold back."

Stone glared at her. Then, with a grunt of exasperation, he wheeled and strode to his horse. Ellie's eyes glittered with disappointment as she watched the retreating back of her trail boss. "I don't know what's got into Arnie. He used to have gumption. Now it seems like he's scared of his own shadow."

McGuire shrugged to himself, unwrapped a hind quarter of fresh beef and began cutting off steaks for the noonday meal. Pinto Gonzales came in from a firewood hunt, dragging a cottonwood branch up to the cooking fires. "I seen some of your pals over there behind the knoll," he said pointing.

McGuire looked sharply. "Hooker's scalp hunters?"

"That's what they looked like to me." His dark face looked worried. For a moment he listened to Ellie Moncrief grinding coffee on the other side of the wagon. "You know what I think? I think we'd be better off somewheres else. It's startin' to come to me that hookin' up with a trail herd wasn't such a good notion after all."

The coffee mill on the far side of the wagon was suddenly silent. Ellie Moncrief circled the letdown table and stood for a moment glaring at the nighthawk. "If you're scared," she told him grimly, "you're free to ride. You can draw your pay when the outfit gets to Dodge."

McGuire, with an elaborate air of indifference, continued to cut and stack the steaks. Then, as the silence was becoming oppressive, one of the swing riders topped a nearby knoll and shouted in alarm, "Boys, they're runnin'!"

Suddenly the cooking fires began to dance to the drumming of hoofs on the hard earth. A dozen wild-eyed steers topped the rise, a quarter of a mile from the wagon, and raced blindly toward the open prairie. Immediately a hundred steers crowded behind the first dozen, and within a matter of seconds the entire herd was pouring over the sea of brown grass. The wagon began to rock. McGuire's stack of cut steaks toppled into the dirt.

Ellie Moncrief stood with her mouth half open, staring in disbelief. "Get me somethin' to ride," McGuire hollered at Gonzales. Then he grabbed the mistress of the Circle-M and heaved her over the sideboards and into the wagon. For the moment she was too stunned to be outraged.

183

Gonzales brought up his own horse and the day wrangler's mount, leaving the wrangler to saddle another animal for himself. McGuire swung aboard the shaggy little roan, his cook apron flying in the wind, and raced toward the point of the herd.

Shorty Eller and Arnie Stone were already shouldering into the leaders. McGuire's stomach seemed to shrink to the size of a hickory nut when he saw how the trail boss was throwing himself at the panic-stricken cattle. The slightest wrong move would mean disaster. A dog hole, a stumbling pony, an unseen outcrop in the grass—there were a hundred ways for a man to die in the van of a stampede. McGuire gritted his teeth and plunged in alongside Stone.

For the next several minutes the crew was caught in a fury of thundering hoofs and choking dust. With the added weight of McGuire and Gonzales throwing themselves at the leaders, the point slowly began to turn. McGuire leaned out of the saddle and savagely kicked the lead steer in the ribs. The big brindle animal flung its head around and glared balefully at the man on horseback. McGuire kicked again, this time driving a pointed toe alongside the animal's ear. The leader grunted and allowed itself to be turned in on the flank of the main stampede.

Within half an hour the main body of the herd had been halted. The animals, calmer now, allowed themselves to be milled in a large circle. The sweating, cursing riders, planted themselves between the cattle and the chuck wagon. As soon as the situation was more calm, Arnie Stone broke away and headed for the wagon.

"Ellie, you all right?"

"Course, I'm all right," she said stiffly, rising up behind the wagon seat. But her face was chalky, and her lips were faintly blue. She swallowed with some difficulty, staring out at the nervous cattle which the hands were slowly hazing back to the trail. "How many head did we lose?"

"Can't tell yet." Arnie wiped his face with a blue bandanna. "Not many. Pretty soon I'll get the boys to round them up. It could of been worse—we had a lot of weight on the point."

"I saw McGuire and Gonzales throwin' their-selves at the leaders," she told him coolly. "Do you still think we ought to turn them over to the bounty hunters?"

The trail boss pulled his head down between his shoulders. Small spots of color appeared in his cheeks. "I saw what they did, but the stampede never would of happened if it hadn't been for them." He leaned wearily on his saddle horn. "This time we was lucky, Ellie—level ground and broad daylight. Next time it could be night, in cut-bank country. Do you think the cook is worth riskin' it?" He rode away before she could answer.

Pinto Gonzales cut away from the herd and rode down the long grade to the wagon. His dark eyes were worried. "Ma'am, have you seen anything of McGuire?"

Ellie shook her head. "Isn't he still with the herd?"

"I couldn't find him. Course, there was a good deal of dust and confusion after we got the cattle turned. I guess he'll be comin' back to the wagon pretty soon now."

But McGuire did not come back to the wagon. At last the swirling dust began to settle and the drovers slowly eased the cattle toward bedground. By ones and twos the hands would ride back for a change of mounts and a cup of coffee. But McGuire did not return.

"Last I seen of him," one drover told Ellie, "he was back in the drag with Rusty Miller. Leastwise I think it was him. Hard to tell, all this dust."

Young Rusty Miller was called to the wagon. "No ma'am," he told Ellie. "I never saw him at all. Never saw much of anything, to tell the truth about it, till after the dust began to settle."

McGuire had disappeared. With anxious faces, the hands scoured the area where the point had been turned, looking for some shred of clothing, a blood-damp patch of ground, something that might point to the place where a man had fallen in front of a thousand head of stampeding cattle.

They found nothing. McGuire had disappeared without a trace.

A grim-faced Hobby Walls, Chief Deputy Sheriff of Marlin County, watched the stampede from a thornbush thicket a mile away. From that distance it didn't look like so much, but Hobby himself had once been a cowman and he could guess what it was like up near the point.

Two grinning possemen rode up from a wooded creek bottom and reined up beside the deputy. "That'll give them a taste of what they can expect from here on in," one posseman commented comfortably, "until they're ready to give up McGuire."

"It may take a spell," the second posseman said. "I know drovers. They can be stubborn."

"Stubborn, but not loco"

Hobby Walls regarded the possemen with distaste. As a matter of fact, he was beginning to find everything about the job distasteful. A gutless sheriff, a frightened citizenry, the blood-sucking possemen—and last, but far from least, an enraged gunslinger. It went against the grain having the county—for the moment, at least—in the hands of a killer like Jeremy Hooker. But that was the way fear worked. The deputy didn't have to like it, but he understood it, because he too was afraid of the gunman. So afraid of him that he would deliberately start a stampede and risk killing innocent men.

"How long you aim to give them to turn over McGuire?" the first posseman asked.

Walls shrugged his heavy shoulders. "We'll wait a while and see how they take it."

The second posseman grinned widely. "You ain't forgettin' how the bounty's to be split, are you? Share and share alike, the three of us."

The deputy cleared his throat and spoke with difficulty. "I ain't forgettin'."

They watched the milling cattle in silence. A great gray blanket of dust rose on a gentle breeze and settled slowly back to the prairie. For a good part of an hour the wagon and much of the herd was lost in the ghostly haze.

They held their positions in the thornbush until early afternoon. By that time the dust had settled. Some of the strays had been rounded up, and the main body of the herd was being worked slowly toward bedground.

There seemed to be a good deal of activity around the wagon, but, at that distance, it was hard to tell what it meant. At last a lone horsebacker rode away from the wagon, pointing due north. "It's the trail boss," Walls told his possemen. "Ride down and head him off, before the other scalp hunters get to him."

The grinning possemen eased their animals out of the thicket and down the long slope toward the main cattle trail. The deputy waited where he was, his hands folded on the saddle horn, his face a mask. At last Arnie Stone broke through the wall of brush, escorted by the two posse-men.

The trail boss's face was pale and angry. "Are you the one that started the stampede?" he said to the deputy.

Hobby Walls moved his shoulders. "Things happen—that's not important now. You know we mean business."

Arnie drew a deep breath. He seemed to be bracing himself for a blow. "I can't help you with what you want. McGuire ain't with the outfit anymore."

The deputy and the two possemen rose straight in their saddles. There was a ringing silence on the brush-strewn knoll. The possemen began to turn ugly, but Walls made a slashing, silencing gesture with one hand. "Don't act the fool, Stone. We know McGuire's with your outfit. We even seen him leave the wagon and help turn the stampede."

"He got lost in the dust, sometime while the herd was millin'."

The deputy's face was like stone. "We'll look for ourselves."

Arnie smiled wearily.

"And if you're lyin', or tryin' to trick us," the deputy went on, "I'll run your herd all the way to the Cap Rock. There won't be nothin' left but hide and bones when we get through with them."

● ● ●

In Tar City, Jeremy Hooker's mood had reached a new viciousness. He sat bolt upright in the hotel chair, glaring at Deputy Hobby Walls. "What do you mean, McGuire's not with the outfit anymore?"

"He ain't with it," Walls said, repeating the statement for the third time. "We started the stampede, like you wanted. When the dust settled, McGuire was gone."

"Gone where?" The gunslinger's face was flushed; he sounded as if he were slowly choking.

"That's what we don't know. There was a lot of dust, he could have sneaked out almost any direction." The deputy sounded more tired than frightened. There was a limit to how much a man would allow himself to be bullied, and Hobby Walls had about reached that limit with Hooker.

Perhaps the gunman detected the change in the lawman's tone. He gazed at him coldly for several seconds, then he quietly drew his .38 and pointed the muzzle at Walls' belt buckle. "If McGuire slips through my fingers, Deputy, I'll kill you. You've got my word on it—and Jeremy Hooker's word is as good as gold."

Hobby Walls licked his dry lips. "I got a feelin' that McGuire will show up, one way or another, before the day is over. Your bounty hunters know he's loose on the prairie. They're sure to run across him before long."

"If they don't?"

Hobby allowed himself a grim little smile. "I didn't come back with McGuire, but I got the next best thing. Wc grabbed McGuire's sidekick, Gonzales."

Jeremy Hooker lay back in his chair. A look—almost a look of peace—settled on his harsh features. "Maybe you've got more sense than I gave you credit for. Where is Gonzales now?"

"In the calaboose. I'm holdin' him on the same warrant that was made out for McGuire."

"You figger McGuire'll try to bust his pal out of the calaboose?"

"He'll try. I've seen McGuire's kind before."

The gunman nodded his head in agreement. "I think maybe you're right—this time." He caressed his double-action .38 affectionately.

Pinto Gonzales was, at the moment, Marlin County's only prisoner. Which was just as well, considering the cramped accommodations. An eight-by-eight rock cell, with an iron barred door facing the downwind side of the wagon yard. A cornshuck mattress, inhabited by countless thousands of bedbugs, lay on the floor against the rock wall. Must be a mighty poor county, Gonzales thought bleakly, that can't afford a better jailhouse than this.

It had been almost six hours since he had gone out to look for McGuire and had blundered into the deputy and the two possemen. Nobody had to tell him that he was being held hostage, although the two possemen had told him just that several times.

Pinto sighed with resignation, hunkered down with his back to the wall and methodically rolled a cigarette. The town was almost in total darkness. The last saloon had gone dark almost three hours ago. The last light in the hotel—the one in Hooker's room—had been out almost as long. The only light that Gonzales could see was a weak one in the wagon yard barn.

Out of the darkness a voice called softly, "Gonzales, can you hear me?"

Pinto froze. "Who is it?"

"Rusty Miller. Missus Moncrief sent me to find out about McGuire. You know what happened to him?"

"No. Where are you?"

"Over here on the dark side of the calaboose."

"How'd you get here, anyhow? Hasn't the deputy got somebody watchin' the calaboose, in case McGuire decides to come prowlin' around?"

"I seen two of them over at the livery barn." There was a grin in the young drover's voice. "Both of them asleep. Possemen, I guess they was." There was a moment of thoughtful silence. Then, "I been studyin' this calaboose, Gonzales. Looks awful solid to me. You got any notion how I could get you out of there?"

"Nothin' short of hitchin' a dray team to the door and pullin' her out by the roots," Gonzales said dryly.

"Will you be all right till tomorrow night?" the youth asked. "Missus Moncrief will want to know."

"It ain't me that Hooker's gunnin' for, it's McGuire. What's this about tomorrow night?"

"Missus Moncrief figgers we can get the herd over the county line before sundown tomorrow. After we get the cattle bedded down, she aims to send part of the crew back to bust you out of here."

"Missus Moncrief is loco!"

The grin was back in Rusty's voice. "That's what the trail boss thinks too. But her mind's made up. She wants you and McGuire back with the outfit. Says it's bad for the Circle-M name, lettin' hardcases like Hooker run off the help. Might be she's right. Anyhow, most of the crew is sidin' with her and against Arnie Stone."

Pinto scowled. "They're willin' to risk their hides for the likes of Willie McGuire?"

"He saved my life. It ain't every day you run across a cook that can cure mad-dog bites."

Pinto gazed up at the dark Texas sky and wondered why he had ever left his native Chihuahua. "I got to go now," Rusty Miller said. "Set easy, Gonzales. I reckon Missus Moncrief aims to save your hide with McGuire's."

The young drover scurried off into the night. Pinto sat for several minutes, unmoving. At last he built himself another smoke and lit it. "Set easy," he said to himself with some asperity.

He didn't much care for the prospect of being caught in the middle of a war between the Circle-M crew and Hooker's tame lawmen. Still, he had to admire the cold-blooded way the mistress of the outfit was going about it. First get the cattle across the county line to comparative safety, *then* see what she could do about her two hands. First things first. It was a line of reasoning that could hardly be argued with, but somehow Gonzales did not find it comforting.

ten

It was near sundown when McGuire reined his borrowed roan into the heavy brush of a creek bottom. Wearily, he climbed down from the saddle, unbitted and loosened the cinch. "What I wish we had," he told the animal, "is maybe a handful of coffee, and somethin' to boil it in."

He searched the wrangler's saddle pockets and found a small emergency ration of jerky. Resignedly, he watered the roan at the brackish stream, then staked the animal in a stand of buffalo grass to graze. "You're better fixed for grub than I am," he said sourly.

McGuire knelt beside the stream to drink, seeing his own reflection in the still water. It was then that he saw that he was still wearing the dirty white apron of a wagon cook. With a grunt of disgust he tore off the offending garment and hurled it into the brush. "I've had a bait of dough-punchin'," he announced grimly to the world at large. "And that goes for female ranch bosses, and shilly-shally trail bosses, and cattle drives in general!"

He washed his face in the cool stream, then sat back on the clay bank, took out his pocketknife and cut off a thin sliver of jerky. For some time he chewed on the leathery, sun-cured meat, washing each mouthful down with a gulp of gyp water. He thought longingly of crusty sourdoughs and fried steaks and hot, bitter coffee. He turned and gazed up at the peacefully grazing roan. "Say what you want to," he said sternly, "but I was a first-class cook. While I lasted." He sighed and lay back in the grass and determinedly dismissed that episode from his mind.

"What I got to do," he said thoughtfully, "is think of a way to get out of this county—out of Texas would be better—without gettin' myself caught by Hooker's scalp hunters."

He had been lucky so far, slipping away from the herd under the blanket of dust. But by this time the bounty hunters must surely realize that he was no longer with the outfit. "Eat yourself a bait of that grass," he told the roan. "We'll start travelin' again soon's the sun goes down."

Horses, it occurred to him, made fine saddle animals but poor conversationalists. It also occurred to him that he missed Gonzales to jaw and argue and pass the time with. Somewhere in the midst of that thought McGuire closed his eyes and was instantly asleep.

When he awoke the creek bottom lay beneath a steely darkness. Stars glittered in a midnight sky. His clothing was wet with dew. Stiff and cold, he shoved himself to his feet. "Hell and damnation," he said half-heartedly, "I ought to of been halfway to Kansas by this time."

He started toward the roan but pulled up sharply, looking startled. There was a fragrance of frying bacon in the air. He raised his head and sniffed like an old he-wolf downwind from a pen of chickens.

McGuire's belly rumbled. His mouth watered at the thought of hot food. Involuntarily, his feet began moving taking him toward the frying bacon. Before long he could see the reddish light of a campfire. The fragrance of boiling coffee mingled with that of bacon.

He was about to call out when a voice in the back of his mind warned, "Wait a minute. Make sure who you're dealin' with."

He continued in the direction of the fire, but slower now, picking his way through the brush with care. A deep male voice was saying, "No two ways about it, he's smarter'n some of us give him credit for bein'. Sneakin' off that way under a cloud of dust."

A younger, shriller voice said bitterly, "A thousand dollars! All lost, because that fool deputy had to go and stampede the cattle."

"No sense to fret about it now," the deep voice said. "Finish up the meat and empty the coffeepot. We still got a chance of collectin' that bounty if we get to Tar City in time."

Bounty hunters! McGuire thought disgustedly. He hunkered down in a patch of dark mullein and studied them carefully. The deep, harsh voice belonged to a part-time wagoner by the name of Bessler; McGuire dimly remembered seeing him in the saloons of Tar City. The other man was young, blond, pasty-faced—McGuire had never seen him before.

Bessler was rumbling on comfortably: "I knew McGuire—know his kind, anyhow. He'll come sneakin' back to Tar City soon's he hears they got his sidekick in the calaboose."

McGuire froze. Gonzales in the calaboose? How could that be?

Bessler obligingly answered his unspoken question. "Sorry day for that Mex that he thought to hook up with a hard luck galoot like McGuire. Like as not that gunslinger'll gun him down, out of pure meanness, whether McGuire shows up or he don't."

The young man laughed—a high-pitched, cackling sound that set McGuire's teeth on edge. "You really figger we got a chance for that money?"

"Long as McGuire's still on the loose we got a chance" Bessler stood up and began kicking out the fire. "Pack the skillet and coffeepot. Quicker we get back to town, better our chances are." He tramped off toward their hobbled saddle animals, leaving the youth to break camp.

Bit by bit McGuire put the picture together in his mind. Somehow Gonzales had allowed the scalp hunters to grab him and lock him in the

198

county jail. No doubt it was all fair and legal, according to Marlin County standards, but what it boiled down to was that Gonzales was being held hostage.

The two bounty hunters rode out of the dark bottom and disappeared in the night. McGuire built himself a cigarette and cursed wearily. That damn Gonzales! Why'd he have to go and get himself caught at a time like this! "Teach him a lesson if I just rode off and left him. I got half a mind to do it," he thought aloud as he climbed into the dew-wet saddle. "If I had any sense, I *would*."

But by that time he already had the roan pointed in the direction of Tar City.

It was an hour past sunup when McGuire raised the pitched roof of the Tar City livery barn. The flinty light of early morning shone mercilessly down on the rolling prairie. A prairie dog sitting on its mound could be seen a mile away. It was the time of day when hawks cut wide circles in the sky, patiently waiting for breakfast to show itself. The time of day when ground squirrels and field-mice and rabbits stayed in their holes, if they had any sense. And it was no time for a man with a bounty on his head to be caught on the open prairie—*if* he had any sense.

McGuire gazed at that distant roof in frustration. He had hoped to slip into town under cover of darkness, but the little roan had lost a shoe sometime during the night, and travel had been a slow business after that. "Well," he thought out loud, "if I ride into town now, in broad daylight, like as not them scalp hunters will shoot me right out of the saddle."

He shoved his hat back and looked up at a circling hawk. He began to understand how the rabbits and fieldmice felt. "Son," he said, stroking the roan's neck, "I got a notion we better locate a place to set and do some thinkin'. Gettin' ourselves drygulched ain't goin' to be any help to Gonzales."

The animal began to favor its off foreleg. Resignedly, McGuire climbed down and began leading. "What I wish," he complained bitterly, "is that Gonzales was back in Chihauhau, where he come from. And I was with him."

They came to a deep-rutted trail that McGuire knew was the main freight road, generally paralleling the cattle trail, to Dodge. On the far side of the road they came upon an arroyo which, in an emergency, might do as cover for a man and his horse. McGuire led the roan down the steep banks of the wash. During the spring rains this gully would most likely be rushing bank-full with muddy water, but now the bottom was sand and weeds.

McGuire gazed bleakly around at the scrawny weeds and the useless patches of sawgrass. "Ain't much here in the way of grub," he told the horse.

He glumly inspected the roan's hoof. Without the shoe, the horse was useless for riding. With a sigh of resignation, he stripped off the saddle and bridle and let the animal wander off down the arroyo looking for food.

The sun was beginning to burn with its accustomed July fury. Without food or water, it would be a long, hot wait till nightfall. Still, McGuire thought with impeccable logic, there were worse things than waiting. Getting yourself shot, for one thing.

He hunkered down with his back against the shady side of the arroyo, built a cigarette and tried to think what he would do when night finally came again and he got to Tar City. *If* he got there. Would Gonzales still be in the town calaboose? Would Hooker, in a fit of rage, use him for target practice?

The morning dragged on. A big land terrapin wandered into the arroyo and trundled past McGuire without so much as a glance in his direction. The sun reached the top of the sky and savagely blasted the prairie, the arroyo, and, in particular, McGuire.

Toward midday a small party of bounty hunters passed along the freight road, heading for Tar City. McGuire was pleased to note that they looked exhausted and evil-tempered.

The afternoon wore on. McGuire, with nothing better to do at the moment, tugged his hat down over his face and dozed. His empty stomach rumbled. He dreamed of cool water and hot food. He dreamed of foaming beer and dance hall girls and free lunch counters. From time to time he would rouse himself and listlessly curse Gonzales.

It was during one of these brief moments of wakefulness that he heard the wagon jolting along the rutted road nearby. McGuire peered over the edge of the arroyo. It was not a freighter or a trail outfit's wagon—a light farm wagon, considerably the worse for wear and need of grease. Probably the rig of some haywire ranch close by, going after supplies in Tar City.

McGuire watched it for some time, then lost interest and settled again in the bottom of the arroyo and continued his fitful dozing. The next thing he heard was a twangy, nerve-grating voice saying, "Set where you are, mister. Start actin' smart and you're good as dead."

McGuire came awake with a start. Cautiously, he shoved his hat back on his head and stared for a moment into the muzzle of an ancient fifteen-shot Henry. "No use grabbin' for your .45," the voice told him. "I got it." The man grinned widely.

At last McGuire tore his gaze away from the muzzle of the rifle and studied the face of the man who held it. He saw little there to comfort him— watery eyes, puckered mouth, patchy whiskers that couldn't quite make up their mind to be a beard. "You the wagoner that passed along the road a while back?"

The man nodded. "Seen your roan come out of the wash. Still had the sweat marks of the saddle pad on him. That struck me queer, so I come back on foot to have a look-see." He grinned again, displaying a remarkably uneven row of speckled teeth. "Your name's McGuire, ain't it? I heard about you—about the bounty, too." He waved the rifle threateningly. "Get on your feet, McGuire. We're goin' to Tar City—and I aim to collect myself that bounty."

As McGuire got to his feet something came over him. It occurred to him that he had had about all the pushing and shoving and threatening that he could use. He was sick of amateur scalp hunters and limp-spined lawmen, not to mention hardcase gunslingers like Jeremy Hooker. "Mister," he told the rifleman with feeling, "you might as well put that rifle down. You ain't never goin' to get your hands on that bounty."

The man blinked rapidly. The beginning of alarm was in his watery eyes. "Head down the wash toward the wagon. And no foolishness, unless you're in a hurry to get shot." He waved his rifle for emphasis. That was a mistake.

With a bull-like roar, McGuire threw himself at the rifleman. He lashed out blindly. The Henry flew in one direction, the man in another. The struggle was over almost before it started. Quickly,

McGuire grabbed his .45 out of the man's waistband and stepped back. He wasn't even short of breath.

From the ground, the man stared up at him with bulging eyes. His mouth worked spasmodically. "Mister, don't kill me! I'm just a cowhand, same as you—I wouldn't of turned you over to that gunslinger!"

McGuire regarded him with disgust. "What I ought to do is shoot you with your own Henry and leave you for the buzzards. And that's what I'd do, except a rifleshot draws too much attention." Then his fit of anger burned itself out. That was the trouble with being hotheaded—you woke up in jail, or with a gunslinger on your tail, and you couldn't even remember how or why it had happened. He pointed the rifle muzzle at the ground and asked wearily, "What's your name?"

The man's Adam's apple bobbed wildly as color returned to his face. "Cotter. Frank Cotter. I run some cattle up by the Duro. "

"Where was you headed when you saw the roan?"

"Tar City. After a load of salt."

McGuire thought for a moment. "All right, Cotter," he said dryly, "I wouldn't want to throw you late. We'll both go to Tar City."

Moving slowly along the rutted freight road, the wagon, with McGuire crouched down behind the driver's seat, raised Tar City within an hour.

Peering through the cracks in the sideboards, he saw that the street was deserted. This came as no surprise. It was a fair example of what a hair-trigger gunslinger like Jeremy Hooker could do to a town.

McGuire pointed his revolver casually at Cotter and said, "You know where the town calaboose is?"

Cotter swallowed hard and nodded.

"That's where you want to go," McGuire told him.

"It'll cause folks to wonder," Cotter said uneasily. "They're used to seein' me put up at the wagon yard when I come to town."

"They'll just have to wonder. In the alley behind the general store is where the calaboose is, and the calaboose is where Gonzales is, so that's where we'll go."

Cotter twisted his head and looked at him worriedly. "Have you thought what you're goin' to do when you get there? The marshal will be watchin' that calaboose, just waitin' for you to show up. So'll the deputy sheriff, most likely, not to mention a pack of possemen and bounty hunters."

McGuire was only too well aware of the dangers of the project, but at the moment he could think of nothing better. Anyway, it had never been his way to ponder over his problems. Charging head-on into the fray, that was more the style of Willie McGuire.

"Hold up a minute," McGuire said suddenly. He pressed his face to the sideboard and squinted at Marshal Frank Hargarty who was just rounding into the street. "Call the marshal over," he said to Cotter. "Tell him you got somethin' here in the wagon that he ought to see."

Cotter paled. "The marshal'd have my hide if I tried a thing like that."

McGuire showed him the muzzle of the .45. "I'll have it if you don't."

With a sickly expression on his face, Cotter raised one hand and called to the lawman. McGuire waited patiently. He would not soon forget the startled expression on Marshal Hargarty's face when he climbed over the wheel and looked down into the wagon box, into the muzzle of McGuire's .45.

"This," McGuire told him, "is what you're goin' to do, Marshal. You're goin' to stay right where you are, while Cotter goes to your office and fetches the key to the jail. Then we'll all go back to the alley and let my sidekick know the town don't want him for a prisoner, after all."

Bertrand Seward was standing behind the plate-glass window of his bank, glaring bleakly out at the almost deserted town, when he saw the Cotter wagon enter Main Street. He knew it was the Cotter wagon because Frank Cotter had borrowed from Seward to buy it. In a perfectly natural way, for men of his calling, he regarded Cotter with a certain interest, to reassure himself that the rancher was in sound health and in condition to settle his legal debts.

The banker was not overly reassured by what he saw. Cotter, alone on the wagon seat, appeared pale and nervous. From time to time he would glance back over his shoulder to look at something in the wagon box. Something—or someone—that Seward could not see because of the sideboards.

Cotter's rig rattled on past the wagon yard, which in itself was rather odd. Cotter habitually left his rig at the yard and did necessary business at the neighboring feed store and saddlery.

As the wagon creaked past the false-fronted bank, Marshal Frank Hargarty, making his customary rounds of the town, stepped into the street from the back alley. Cotter again turned nervously to peer over his shoulder. With his face curiously set and grim, Cotter braked the wagon and called to the marshal.

On the face of it, this little scene was perfectly normal and harmless. Yet, the banker's concern began to mount. He began to look for tangible reasons for Cotter's faintly curious actions and appearance, for anything that affected a bank customer affected Bertrand Seward.

As the marshal approached the wagon he suddenly pulled up short and looked startled. His right hand moved quickly, almost as if he were grabbing for the revolver that rode middling low on Frank Hargarty's right thigh. But the hand froze in midair. After a moment Hargarty let it hang stiffly at his side, and he continued on to the wagon.

The banker was fascinated. He moved closer to the window.

Now, with what appeared to be great reluctance, Hargarty climbed onto the rear wheel of Cotter's wagon and looked into the box. What he saw did not appear to give him comfort. Now, both Hargarty and Cotter were looking into the wagon box. Their expressions were grim.

Suddenly the scene became even more puzzling. Frank Cotter set his brake and wrapped his lines and climbed down over the front wheel. He walked away from the wagon. Bertrand Seward was tempted to step out to the sidewalk in order to better observe what was going on. But he resisted the temptation and moved instead to the edge of the window from which vantage point he saw Cotter disappear around the corner of Medford's General Store.

The banker's forehead was wrinkled. Unmistakable concern shone in his eyes. In the back of Medford's General Store was where the marshal had his office—and that was where Cotter appeared to be headed. Seward hesitated only for a moment—then, with a grunt of irritation, he quickly locked the bank's front door.

He left the building by the back door, locking it behind him. Within a short time he was telling his suspicions to Deputy Sheriff Hobby Walls.

Pinto Gonzales was dozing on the floor of the rock calaboose when the wagon rounded into the alley. He got slowly to his feet and moved to the barred door. An instinct, developed over years of riding with Willie McGuire, was immediately alert. There was something about the set of the marshal's jaw, the paleness of the driver's face. A ripple of anxiety went up Gonzales' back.

This was not an unfamiliar sensation to Gonzales; he had experienced it many times before—usually just before a barroom brawl, and always in connection with McGuire. This was what he found puzzling now; McGuire was nowhere in sight. He was not even within a day's ride of Tar City, as far as Gonzales knew.

The wagon moved directly toward the rock calaboose and braked to a stop in front of the door. The marshal did not speak—he stared angrily into the far distance. The driver glanced down at the prisoner and swallowed hard. That was when McGuire—appearing bigger than life and twice as loud—rose up behind the wagon seat and hollered, "We come to let you out of there, Gonzales. I bet you're surprised to see me, ain't you?"

Gonzales groaned to himself. "McGuire, what're

you doin' here? Don't you know the deputy and his scalp hunters're watchin' this calaboose?"

"Son," McGuire told him accusingly, "you just don't appreciate a thing I do for you. Well, I aim to get you out of there, whether you like it or not. Look here . . ." He grinned widely. "The marshal here give us the key to the calaboose." Waving the key in one hand, he started climbing over the sideboard.

Gonzales started to shout a warning. It was too late. At that moment Deputy Hobby Walls stepped out of the back door of Medford's General Store, followed by two possemen and banker Bertrand Seward. The deputy was armed with a choke-barrel scatter gun, the possemen with rifles. "Move another inch, McGuire," the deputy said coldly, "and you're a dead wagon cook."

For a moment McGuire looked amazed. His scheme that had seemed so ingenious now appeared to be falling apart like a soddie hut in a rainstorm. For a few seconds he considered his position and weighed his chances. If the deputy fired his scatter gun, like as not he would kill Cotter and the marshal, as well as McGuire. But McGuire had the uneasy feeling that this, to Deputy Walls, was a matter of small importance.

The lawman spoke again, and this time his voice took a steely edge. "Let your gun go, McGuire"

McGuire sighed and dropped his battered .45 into the dust.

"Now the keys," the deputy told him.

McGuire obediently dropped the keys to the calaboose and climbed down to the ground. The stonelike face of Deputy Walls relaxed. He allowed himself a small smile. "McGuire, I reckon I ought to say much oblige for ridin' right into my hands this way. You've just made me a rich man." He nodded to his possemen. "Lock him up. I'll go tell Hooker."

eleven

Jeremy Hooker, stripped to his union suit in the sweltering heat of the hotel room, allowed a look of satisfaction to relax his normally grim expression. "You've got McGuire in the calaboose? There's no mistake?"

"Not this time," the deputy told him. "He rode right into my hands, lookin' to bust his sidekick out of jail. Just the way you figgered."

A rare expression touched the corners of the gunslinger's mouth. He smiled. "Good. Get your bounty from the banker." He closed his eyes and thought for a moment. "Leave the jail keys with me, then get out. I've got some thinkin' to do. I've waited a long time for this moment, and I want it to be just right."

He sat in silence for some time, his eyes closed, no trace of a smile left on his face. "McGuire's in the calaboose," he said aloud to the empty room. "There's nothin' to fret about. No need to hurry. A job that's worth doin' is worth doin' right . . ." And if your business was killing, that time-worn saying was doubly true.

It would be an easy thing simply to have McGuire brought to him, and kill him on the spot. But that kind of killing would never do. Not, if your name was Jeremy Hooker. Not, if you valued your reputation. And in Hooker's business, a man's reputation was as good as his life. If word ever got around that Jeremy Hooker was afraid to meet a common wagon cook in a fair gunfight . . .

The mere thought of such an improbability caused beads of sweat to break out on the gunman's forehead. No, merely killing McGuire was not enough. Too many people were watching—young, would-be gunslingers with reputations of their own to make. "Did you hear about Jeremy Hooker? Drygulched a wagon cook that busted his leg. Must be that Hooker's gettin' old."

No, that definitely would not do.

It would have to have every appearance of a fair fight. Better yet, it had to appear that every advantage favored McGuire.

Hooker opened his eyes and stared blankly. Very faintly, he smiled. McGuire himself had, with his own peculiar genius, set the stage for his own death. Thanks to him, Hooker was now laid up in bed with a broken leg, a cripple.

The gunslinger stared fiercely into space. He could see it now—the crippled gunfighter hobbling through the dusty street on crutches to meet the enemy. Yes, that was the kind of thing that maintained reputations and created legends.

Hooker pounded on the floor with the barrel of his revolver. Within a matter of seconds the little hotel owner had scurried up the rickety stairway. "Get me Doc Mulley," the gunman said with startling good humor. "And a pair of crutches. And a pair of hands to help me down to the street."

An hour later Jeremy Hooker stood on a pair of Doc Mulley's crutches, studying himself in the scaling mirror over the washstand. He was fully dressed, down to the chamois skin vest with the pocket holsters. For some minutes he practiced walking on the crutches, thumping back and forth across the room before the bugging eyes of Doc Mulley and two possemen. The slit leg of Hooker's trousers flapped like a broken wing, but the gunman did not mind. It rather added to the drama of the situation, he thought.

"Get out," he told Mulley and the possemen. "Come back in half an hour and help me down to the street."

When he was alone in the room, Hooker again took up his position in front of the mirror. He shoved his revolver into the pocket holster and began practicing his draw.

The first few draws were distressingly slow. Gunfighting on crutches was going to be more difficult than he had anticipated. For perhaps ten minutes he worked at adjusting his weight on the twin crutches, grabbing the .38 out of the holster pocket and snapping it at the mirror. The line of his mouth became grim. Rivulets of sweat rolled down his face and dropped from the point of his chin. Shift, grab, snap. Shift, grab, snap.

Because of the crutches, his shoulders were raised higher than normal. He propped himself against the washstand, pulled up the vest and tightened it with a buckskin thong in the back. He repositioned himself and tried to draw again.

This time it was better. Not good—far from it— but better. If he had known how inept McGuire was with firearms, he would have been satisfied. As it was, he continued to practice the draw. Shift, grab, snap. Each time the lean fingers shot slantwise across his chest a little faster, the butt slapped into his palm with something like his old-time speed.

At last he was satisfied. He selected five cartridges from his belt, wiped them clean on his bandanna and slipped them into the cylinder. Once again he hammered on the floor, and once again the possemen appeared this time to help him down to the street.

McGuire and Gonzales regarded each other with mutual disgust. "How," McGuire demanded for the dozenth time, "could you be so hammerheaded as to get yourself throwed in the calaboose?"

Gonzales smiled wearily. There was no use arguing against McGuire's peculiar kind of logic. "How I got here ain't the important thing right now. I'm here, and so're you. And, if I don't miss my guess, we'll soon have company."

"Company?"

"Jeremy Hooker. You ain't forgettin' what this fandango is all about, are you?"

McGuire grabbed the barred door and rattled it distractedly. "What're you talkin' about? Hooker's laid up with a busted leg."

"I don't figger a busted leg's goin' to stop him now." Gonzales sighed. "I don't figger *any*thing's goin' to stop him, unless . . ." He told his side-kick about the brief talk he'd had with Rusty Miller.

McGuire brightened for a moment. "There you are! Everything's goin' to be fine. The Circle-M crew will bust us out of here." Suddenly he sobered. "You don't figger the youngster was makin' it up, do you?"

"No, I don't think that. I figger it'll just be too late to do us any good."

McGuire had been in the calaboose for almost an hour during which time he had noticed a great deal of activity between the wagon yard and the Tar City Hotel. He wasn't actually worried until he saw Doc Mulley headed for the hotel with a pair of hickory crutches under one arm.

Frank Cotter rounded the corner of the general store and headed for the wagon yard where he had taken his team. After a moment's hesitation, he stepped down from the plankwalk and started for the calaboose. McGuire was not comforted to see that the haywire rancher was smiling widely.

"If you recollect any prayers, McGuire, you better start sayin' them now. Won't be long before Jeremy Hooker'll have you laid out for plantin'."

McGuire eyed the rancher with growing uneasiness. "What're you talkin' about? Hooker ain't in no shape for fightin'."

"All depends on who he's goin' up against." Cotter grinned toothily, remembering the rough treatment that he had received at the hands of McGuire. With an unpleasant chuckle, he wheeled and continued on to the barn.

McGuire sank dejectedly to the floor of the calaboose and worriedly built a cigarette. "You figger there's anything to what Cotter says? A man wouldn't go startin' a fight on crutches, would he?"

"He might," Gonzales shrugged, "if his name's Jeremy Hooker. Like Cotter says—it all depends."

McGuire sighed heavily and lit a cigarette. "You don't figger a gunslinger'd shoot a man down without givin' him a chance, do you?"

Gonzales grunted. "Not Hooker. It would be the worst thing he could do. Bad for his reputation."

For a moment McGuire looked vaguely hopeful. "That's right. He couldn't just shoot me down. He'll have to give me a gun."

"He'll give you a gun," Gonzales said glumly. "I don't know as I'd call that much of a chance."

The shadow of the calaboose stretched darkly in front of the barred door. "Less than an hour till sundown," Gonzales said. "Maybe the Circle-M crew will get here in time, after all."

McGuire smoked an endless chain of cigarettes, wistfully recollecting the brawls and fandangos that had been so much a part of his life. The dance hall girls he had known. The roaring trail towns. He didn't actually believe that Ellie Moncrief would risk getting her crew shot up just to set loose a wagon cook. But it was the only hope he had, and he clung to it.

There was some kind of commotion near the hotel. McGuire and Gonzales got to their feet. Suddenly Doc Mulley appeared on the plank sidewalk at the side of the hotel. Then the deputy, Hobby Walls, and his two possemen. They were all hovering around a fifth figure. McGuire felt a cold breath on the back of his neck—the fifth man was Jeremy Hooker.

Gonzales took a deep breath and let it whistle between his teeth. He shot a look of sympathy at his partner. McGuire, he knew, had as much nerve as the next man, but he was no gunfighter. The crutches made no difference at all. Gonzales mentally crossed himself. His friend was as good as dead.

Hooker stood erect at the end of the sidewalk, braced on his crutches. He looked at the calaboose for several seconds, his face expressionless; only his eyes were hot and alive. The slit leg of his trousers flapped listlessly in the idle wind, revealing the bulky white cast on his leg. Hobby Walls and the possemen hurried to his assistance as he cautiously let himself down from the plank sidewalk, but the gunslinger kept them at a distance with a burning glance.

"Handles them crutches pretty good," Gonzales said resignedly.

McGuire said nothing. He too was resigned for whatever was to come. He absently admired the gleaming .38 in the pocket of Hooker's chamois skin vest. Walls, walking slowly beside the gun-slinger, carried a second revolver in his hand—McGuire's own .45.

Suddenly Gonzales frowned. "Do you hear somethin'?"

McGuire looked at him. "What?"

"Horses, I think. I ain't sure yet."

They were silent for a moment, listening. Then they heard it, the sound of distant hoofs. Hooker and his party heard it too. The gunslinger snapped a few words over his shoulder and the two posse-men immediately headed toward the barn at a run.

McGuire glanced at his sidekick. "The Circle-M crew?"

"Maybe. We'll soon know."

One of the possemen came loping back from the livery barn, hollering something to the deputy. A scattering of townsmen and loafers came scurrying out of the barn, some of them taking up fighting positions behind water troughs and straw piles or whatever they could find. Gonzales regarded the sudden flurry of action with detachment. "Looks like," he said dryly, "that Missus Moncrief got the herd bedded down a little early today."

McGuire grasped the iron bars and watched the scene with fascination. The gunslinger suddenly began snarling and snapping orders at the deputy. Horsebackers entered the far end of the street. McGuire recognized the angry face of Arnie Stone, and the red thatch of Rusty Miller. Then, for a moment, Ellie Moncrief swept into view. McGuire was mildly outraged to see that she was riding astride, like a man. "If a woman ain't got a sidesaddle, or maybe a buggy to ride in," he muttered sourly, "then she ought to stay home."

Ellie shouted something to her trail boss, and Arnie, with obvious reluctance, motioned for the crew to follow him. They disappeared behind the line of buildings.

For a moment everything was unnaturally quiet. Then there was a lone rifle shot from the direction of the barn. Gonzales groaned to himself. "There starts the war. And here we are, caught in the middle."

Marshal Frank Hargarty lunged into view from behind the Drover Saloon and stood for a moment in indecision, looking at the calaboose. Without much hope, Gonzales shouted, "Marshal, let us out of here before the real shootin' starts!"

The marshal slowly took a heavy jail key out of his pocket. He could see that, once the shooting started, the calaboose would be a very dangerous place to be locked up in. He took a few hesitant steps toward the jail. Almost immediately Jeremy Hooker wheeled on his crutches and snarled, "The prisoners stay where they are, Marshal!"

Hargarty quickly retreated. Another rifle shot sounded near the wagon yard, and this time Gonzales saw the plume of gunsmoke drifting up from the barn loft. The shot was followed almost immediately by a flurry of fire from the other end of the alley.

McGuire grabbed the bars and shook them in frustration. "I wish I could see what's goin' on!"

Gonzales knew what was going on. The deputy's possemen and assorted scalp hunters had gathered in the vicinity of the wagon yard; Ellie Moncrief and her crew were taking positions at the other end of the alley. The calaboose stood in between. It was only a matter of time before bullets started to come through the barred door.

Jeremy Hooker, unassisted, climbed back to the sidewalk and disappeared inside the hotel. There was a short spell of silence, then another flurry of gunfire. A bullet smashed against the rock wall of the calaboose. "Maybe this ain't such a bad place to be, after all," McGuire said thoughtfully. Then a bullet slammed into the jail through the barred door, missing McGuire's head by inches. "On the other hand," he admitted, moving as far from the door as possible, "I could be wrong."

The firing became sporadic. From time to time a bullet would crash against the stone calaboose, and another one burned in through the doorway. Luckily, McGuire and Gonzales had already decided that in front of the doorway was not a healthy place to be.

There seemed to be a great deal of activity at the far end of the street, but it was hard to see anything from the corner of that rock calaboose. "Hell's afire!" McGuire complained. "We might as well be prairie dogs in our holes, for all we can see in this rock jailhouse."

Suddenly the firing from the wagon yard seemed to be getting heavier, while at the other end of the street it was still fitful and unconcentrated. McGuire risked taking a quick look through the barred doorway. What he saw puzzled him. "Gonzales, what do you make out of this?"

Gonzales reluctantly took a quick look. Hands from the Circle-M herd seemed to be scurrying aimlessly from one place to another. He recognized the red head of Rusty Miller, and the giant figure of Arnie Stone. "I ain't sure," he said worriedly, "but it looks like they're gettin' ready to charge the calaboose."

McGuire looked again, scowling. "It don't look like a charge to me."

"They're gettin' set with rifles on both sides of the alley. Coverin' fire, they call it. Wasn't you ever a soldier?"

"Nope. I was just a sprout when the States was fightin'. Then came the Indian wars, but I never figgered me and the Indians was all that mad at each other."

They continued to watch, taking care to stay in the shadows as much as possible. A lanky figure that McGuire recognized as Matchstick, the day wrangler, streaked across a piece of open space and fell to the ground behind a fire barrel. Shorty Eller followed him and dropped near the blacksmith shop, behind the steel blade of a heavy breaking plow.

"There!" Gonzales said suddenly. Arnie Stone entered the alleyway from between two buildings, leading a team of heavy dray horses. McGuire whistled softly in admiration. "Now there's somethin' that might just work—if somebody can get that team close enough to hook onto this door. Where you reckon they got the work horses?"

"Unhooked them from somebody's dray wagon, I expect," Gonzales grunted.

The possemen at the wagon yard realized what the horses were for; one lunge from that heavy work team would pull out the jail door and probably a good part of the rock wall besides. The firing from the livery barn became heavier. The

Circle-M riders opened fire with their rifles, and Arnie Stone led the team into the hail of bullets.

McGuire shook his head in wonder. "The trail boss has got grit, you got to give him that much."

"He's loco," Gonzales said under his breath. "Or else Ellie Moncrief put him up to this stunt, which is more likely."

Bullets kicked up geysers of dirt in the alley as Arnie zigzagged between them, hauling on the reluctant animals. It occurred to McGuire that he hadn't seen Ellic for some time, but the main part of his attention was focused on Arnie Stone's progress toward the calaboose.

Every man in the Circle-M crew seemed to be firing in the direction of the wagon yard. I wonder who's watching the cattle? Gonzales thought to himself. The possemen from the livery barn were returning the fire, but the sound of bullets snapping about their heads did not improve their marksmanship.

Arnie Stone threw himself to the ground a short distance from the calaboose. He uncoiled a length of heavy log chain and passed it between the bars of the door. "Hook this onto the door close to one of the hinges!"

Gonzales had already grabbed the chain and was lashing it to the bottom cross bar. "By God," he said in disbelief, "we might get out of here yet!"

When the chain was made fast to the door, the

trail boss looked at McGuire. "McGuire, there's somethin' I want from you!"

McGuire stared at him. "This ain't no time to stop and hold a conversation!"

"If I get you out of this jam, I want your word you'll leave this outfit."

"Stone, you're loco! I already quit the outfit, right after the stampede!"

"I want your word!"

"Goddamit, Stone, did you risk your hide just to come up here and chew the fat? I give you my word!"

The trail boss hesitated as the firing from the far end of the alley became heavier. Suddenly he turned, picked up a rock and hurled it at the dray horses. The heavy animals lunged in their collars, the chain snapped taut. Bits of mortar and rock ricocheted about the walls of the calaboose as the door began to give. Rock began to crack and break. Suddenly, with a crack like thunder, the horses broke the steel door free of its stone moorings. They fled down the alley in panic, dragging the door and part of the wall with them.

McGuire was deeply impressed by what had happened. For once he could think of nothing to say. Gonzales grabbed him and gave him a shove out of the ruined calaboose. That was when Jeremy Hooker rounded the corner of the hotel on his crutches and stood for a moment, looking at them. Looking, and grinning.

For perhaps two seconds he stood there, grinning as if his face were breaking. From the wagon yard a few rifles continued to fire, and at the other end of the alley the Circle-M men were firing at a heavy rate. A stray bullet kicked up dust inches from the gunslinger's foot. He didn't seem to notice.

McGuire and Gonzales stepped out of the rubble that had been the calaboose. Arnie Stone pulled himself to his feet and unconsciously started to brush himself off. Suddenly he froze, his right hand almost touching the butt of his gun. Hooker still hadn't moved. He stood there for all to see, waiting for the trail boss to make the first move.

At that moment Deptuy Sheriff Hobby Walls and one of his possemen rounded into view. Each of them held an arm of a struggling Ellie Moncrief. She was spitting like a bobcat, squirming and clawing at the two unhappy lawmen. How they had got their hands on her, McGuire didn't know. While all her crewmen were busy covering Arnie Stone, most likely.

Somehow she broke the posseman's grip for a moment; before he could move she had clawed him across the face, leaving five red furrows the length of his cheek. In a strangely detached way, McGuire had to admire that kind of spirit. Like a high-bred colt before the breaking hands went to work on it. She would make somebody a good woman . . . if a man could tame her.

Hooker was still standing there, erect between his crutches, waiting for Stone to grab his .45, if that was what he had in mind. But Arnie didn't make his move. Cautiously, he moved his hand away from his gun.

Hooker nodded his smiling approval. "All right, trail boss. If you don't aim to fight, unbuckle your gunbelt and let it drop."

Arnie swallowed convulsively, as if a bone had stuck in his throat. He began unbuckling the belt.

Ellie stared at him, her eyes flashing. She didn't even look at the posseman when he grabbed her free arm. "Arnie, do something!"

McGuire glanced at Gonzales, and Gonzales shrugged. They had no strong feelings one way or another about the trail boss, but they could appreciate the bind he was in. If he moved toward his gun he was as good as dead. Possibly he was faster with firearms than Willie McGuire, but he was no match for Jeremy Hooker. Arnie dropped the belt and .45 into the dust.

It was the practical, manlike thing to do. McGuire or Gonzales would have done the same thing if they had been in the trail boss's place. But Ellie didn't see it as a man would see it. All she could see was that Arnie had been invited to defend his own honor, the honor of the outfit, even the honor of the woman he loved. And he had declined.

Jeremy Hooker chuckled quietly—a rare sound that not many men ever heard. "That's the ticket, trail boss. Now just step down the alley a ways, slow and easy, and tell your hands to stop shootin'. Or maybe the lady gets hurt."

Ellie lunged against the hold of her captors. "Arnie, help me!"

It was a wail of bitterness and disappointment. Arnie glanced at her and then looked away.

Deputy Walls was already loping toward the wagon yard to stop the shooting from that end of the alley. Stone, his face pale and drawn, began moving in the opposite direction. Isolated riflemen continued to fire for several minutes—a war once started was not so easy to stop. But at last an uneasy silence settled on Tar City; the smell of gunsmoke was heavy on the summer air.

Hooker, in high good humor, rested on his crutches and grinned at McGuire. "Won't be long now, McGuire. But I want the town to see this. The drovers, too. I don't want it said that Jeremy Hooker took advantage."

McGuire studied the gunslinger warily. He could see how it was going to be—how it was meant to be from the beginning—and nothing he could do would stop it. He said resignedly, "Tell your boys to let go of Missus Moncrief, Hooker. I'll fight you. That's what you want, ain't it?"

The gunslinger looked surprised that McGuire was stepping so docilely into his trap. He shot a quick look at Ellie Moncrief, then looked back at McGuire. A kind of wry amusement looked out of those pale eyes. This was something he hadn't counted on—a bonus, sort of. It hadn't occurred to him that everything between the widow and her wagon cook might not be purely business. Well . . . He seemed to shrug without actually moving. There was, he guesed, no accounting for the ways of women.

A few townsmen and would-be bounty hunters, cautiously entering the alley from the wagon yard, heard Hooker say in his dry, sardonic tone, "A man's got a right to satisfaction. You don't deny that, do you, McGuire?"

Some of the Circle-M hands approached in time to see McGuire shrug his big shoulders. "You'll get satisfaction, Hooker. Tell your boys to let Missus Moncrief go."

"All in good time," the gunslinger told him cheerfully. He turned to Marshal Frank Hargarty, who was standing unhappily at the rear of the hotel. "Clear everybody out of the stores. I want the whole town to see this. I want it known from one end of Texas to the other that Jeremy Hooker gives a man a fair chance." He turned his false smile back on McGuire. "The whole town for a witness—you couldn't ask for anything fairer than that, could you?"

A lot of things sprang to mind, but McGuire merely shrugged. Nothing he could say could help him now. Strangely, the idea of dying didn't frighten him. He was too tired for that. He couldn't remember the last time he had had hot food or a decent night's sleep. A cup of hot coffee, black as a banker's heart, that was what he would like to have right now.

Gonzales nudged his partner and hissed from the side of his mouth. "Might be it ain't too late to save your hide. I've seen these gunsharks before—they like to see a man beg. Could be he'd even let you off with a shot through the leg, to settle up for the one you busted for him."

McGuire thought about it. A bullet through the kneecap. Somehow, it didn't sound like such a good bargain. Anyway, in a lifetime of floating from one job to another, he had never got the habit of begging. He looked at Gonzales with a grin that he didn't feel. "What the hell, this might be my lucky day. How do you know his gun won't misfire? Stranger things have happened."

Gonzales couldn't think of one offhand. "Better to be lame and alive, the way I see it, than to be stretched out with a bullet through your gizzard. Anyhow, a woman ain't worth gettin' yourself shot for."

McGuire was startled by his partner's last statement. "What do you mean, a woman?"

"I seen the way the widow's been lookin' at you, and you at her. She's a prideful woman. And a handsome one—I give you that. But she ain't worth dyin' for.'"

McGuire glared at his sidekick in exasperation. "You don't know what you're talkin' about!"

"Think about it. There still may be time."

McGuire did think about it. It was a disconcerting idea, that he might be throwing himself away because of a prideful woman. Or a handsome one, even.

McGuire glanced in Ellie Moncrief's direction. She was staring at him wide-eyed. He had seen that look before—after he had gone through the rigamarole of madstone practice, with Rusty Miller. It was a possessive look, and maybe something else besides. He didn't like it now any more than he had then. "You know somethin', Gonzales," he said under his breath, "I just got an unsettlin' notion that she thinks I'm standin' up to Hooker on account of her."

Gonzales cocked one dark eye at him. "Ain't you?"

"Hell and damnation, I ain't *that* loco!"

But the fact remained that the widow was there, and he was here, waiting docilely for his own execution—and he didn't know just why he was doing it.

twelve

The Circle-M hands had gathered warily behind their trail boss, in front of the ruined calaboose. Townsmen, loafers, casual drifters, and former bounty hunters gathered near the plank sidewalk behind the Tar City Hotel. Strangely enough, everybody except McGuire and Gonzales was still armed—even Arnie Stone had recovered his gunbelt and buckled it on.

The larger war, it seemed, was over. The general hostility had now boiled down to the original antagonism between McGuire and the gunslinger.

Hooker glanced at Deputy Walls. "Is everybody out of the stores?"

Walls nodded. He was still carrying McGuire's .45 in his hand.

"And off the street?"

"Everybody I could find is here." Including three saloon girls, a Chinese cook from the Tar City cafe, a nervous little traveling peddler, and a visiting gambler from Ellsworth. Together with the townsmen and Circle-M hands they made up a sizable crowd. Jeremy Hooker turned on his crutches and looked them over. He appeared to be satisfied.

"Is there anybody here that ain't heard what this is all about?"

The crowd shifted feet, scratched itself and gazed blankly at the gunslinger. "A while back," Hooker started, in the dry tone of a traveling lecturer, "I was in the Drover Saloon takin' a hand of poker when he . . ." He lifted his left crutch and pointed it at McGuire. "The wagon cook started a fandango, breakin' up the saloon's furniture and a considerable stock of whiskey, and bustin' my leg besides." He paused and searched the faces of his audience. The crowd nodded to show that it knew what was expected of it.

"Busted my leg," Hooker said coldly. None of his earlier good humor was evident now. He was cool and quiet and deadly. "Well, the marshal here did what he could, I guess. He locked McGuire up for the night and made him pay for the damage to the saloon." The gunslinger paused again and regarded his audience. "But nobody paid for my busted leg. That don't sound fair, does it?"

The crowd moved its head from one side to the other.

"It *wasn't* fair. There ain't nothin' fair about it when a man can bust another's leg and get off scott free. I say I've got a natural-born right to satisfaction."

The crowd nodded.

Hooker rested on his crutches and breathed deeply. He looked satisfied with the way things were going. "That," he told his listeners, "is why we're here. Me for satisfaction, you to witness that everything's fair and square."

Ellie Moncrief suddenly shouted, "You can't let this go on! It's murder!"

The crowd didn't move, or look in her direction, or bat an eye. Hooker went on as though she had never spoken. "The fuss is between me and McGuire, and I say we ought to settle it like men of honor."

The crowd nodded eagerly. Hooker turned to the deputy and said, "Give him his gun."

Deputy Walls started moving toward McGuire, holding his .45 out to him. Gonzales watched his partner tensely, hoping for a miracle. McGuire didn't move. He looked dazed. His hand reached out to take the revolver.

Suddenly Gonzales hollered at the gunslinger. "I don't reckon you'd be in such a big hurry to fight if you didn't have that fancy Colt in your pocket!"

The gunslinger blinked. He looked at Gonzales with a faintly startled expression. The crowd turned its head and glared at him. Even McGuire stared at him with disapproval.

Gonzales was as surprised as anyone by his outburst. It was just that the little hawkbill revolver in Hooker's holster pocket looked so clean and cool and deadly, and McGuire's much abused .45 had looked kind of old and sad beside it. Uncomfortably, he looked around at the crowd, at Ellie, at Arnie Stone. They all seemed to be waiting for him to say something else, to somehow justify his outburst.

"Well," he said defensively to Hooker, "it's the truth, ain't it? That gun of yours, the fanciest model in the catalogue, I bet. Must of cost plenty. Been petted and pampered like a spotted colt, if I'm any judge. I bet you never hammered staples in a fencepost with *that* gun."

Gonzales glared fiercely at the stunned faces. "Well," he demanded again, "ain't it the truth? Look at the two guns. *Then* tell me if this is a fair fight, like Hooker claims!"

The gunslinger's face had gone slightly pale. He wheeled on one crutch and looked at the massed faces. He could see that Gonzales' suspicions had gone to work. They regarded the two guns in silence. There was doubt in their eyes.

Somewhere, far behind Hooker's eyes, anger flickered like distant lightning. He drew his double-action Colt from his pocket holster and handed it to the deputy. "I don't want it said that Jeremy Hooker took advantage."

He took McGuire's own .45 and slid it into the smooth pocket of his vest without looking at it. Dumbly, McGuire allowed the deputy to place the little Colt in his hand. It lay there, dark and deadly, as cold as a snake. His own holster was too big for the .38, and after a moment of indecision he thrust in into his waistband. It didn't matter.

He simply did not have the knack with guns.

When McGuire put the revolver in his waistband, the crowd sighed. There was a certain finality to the sound. That, it seemed to say, was the end of it. The beginning of the end, anyhow. McGuire let his glance touch Ellie Moncrief for just a moment. It seemed to him that she was burning with a strange fire. Her eyes were too bright for comfort.

Gonzales looked merely sad. He and McGuire had come a long way together, but the trail had narrowed down to this. It was the end.

McGuire himself felt faintly ridiculous, like the first time he cinched on a cook apron. He found it hard to believe that he was actually expected to draw against Jeremy Hooker, busted leg or not. He found himself half-waiting for somebody to laugh at the last minute, and it would all turn out to be a dose of roughhouse humor.

But nobody laughed. The silence was suddenly oppressive; even the prairie wind was still. The shadow of the shattered calaboose was long and dark. In a few minutes the sun would be setting, but McGuire had no notion of ever seeing it.

Hooker seemed perfectly relaxed and comfortable between his crutches. He stood for several seconds without moving. At last he said, "Make your grab, McGuire. When it's over I don't want your partner tellin' folks I tried to trick you."

237

The depressing thing was, McGuire thought to himself, that it was all so useless and foolish. He didn't *have* to die; he could simply turn and walk away. Hooker wouldn't shoot him in the back. Then, suddenly, it came to him in a flash of crystal clarity that he would do just that. To hell with Hooker and his tender pride. Walk away. It was that simple.

At that moment Hooker's hand started for his gun. After having discovered the solution to his dilemma, there was nothing McGuire could do about it.

Of course, he should have known. Hooker would never have drawn first against a nobody like Willie McGuire. That would have been bad for his reputation. It would have made him the laughingstock of every cowtown between the Bravo and Montana. It was apparent to the waiting crowd that Hooker was merely toying with him, tricking him into making the first draw.

McGuire realized dully what had happened, but by that time it was much too late. He had already fumbled the little .38 out of his waistband. There he stood, with a modern, well-kept instrument of death in his hand. And Hooker, leaning on his left crutch after the false start, still allowed both arms to dangle at his sides. Not until McGuire had acutally raised the .38 did Hooker make his move.

It was almost too fast for the eye to catch. An

electric thrill went through the crowd as the battered .45 sprang into the gunslinger's hand. The hammer snapped back as if by magic. The muzzle swept up in a blurr, dead center on McGuire's chest. All this while McGuire was fumbling striving to find the trigger on the .38.

But it didn't really matter what he did now. He had made the first draw; no jury in the world would fault Hooker for protecting himself. A smile of furious satisfaction tilted the corners of the gunslinger's mouth. After all his days of pain and humiliation, this was the moment he had waited for. The act of squeezing the trigger was a moment that he had lived over and over in his mind, but this in no way lessened the pleasure. His pale eyes glittered. With an infinitesimal little sigh he added the last bit of pressure to the trigger. Nothing happened. There was not even a snap to indicate that the hammer had fallen on a faulty cartridge.

The hammer had not, in fact, fallen on anything at all. It had frozen into position alongside Hooker's thumb. The gunslinger looked as if he couldn't believe it. He added more pressure, squeezing until the muzzle began to quiver. The hammer would not move.

The eyes of the crowd were fixed hypnotically on McGuire. They waited tensely for the explosion and that instant of violence that would snuff out a man's life.

The moment didn't come. The faces were blank with disbelief. They had witnessed the fastest, deadliest draw imaginable, and yet McGuire had not fallen.

Of all those present only Gonzales realized immediately what had happened. For years the revolver had absorbed all kinds of abuse and suffered all kinds of indignities at the hands of Willie McGuire. Pounding staples into fence-posts. Cracking the ironlike shells of pecans and black walnuts. To Gonzales, it seemed only reasonable that the much mistreated weapon would show some sign of contrariness when it was finally called upon to perform its primary function, which was killing. Perhaps dirt or grease, or even sourdough batter, had found its way into some of the revolver's vital working parts. Whatever the reason, the hammer was frozen. The weapon was useless. The deliverer of death was impotent.

From the time that McGuire had fumbled the .38 out of his waistband to the time that Hooker had squeezed the trigger on the .45, perhaps half a second had passed—a long time in a gunfight. It took McGuire another half a second to find the .38's trigger, and still another half a second to realize that something—he didn't know what—was wrong.

For a puzzled instant he held his fire—in a gunfight, the same as committing suicide.

But, as McGuire had wistfully wished earlier, this was indeed his lucky day. Nothing, it seemed, could budge the hammer on the .45. Neither sweat nor strength nor prayer. All of McGuire's problems were suddenly childishly simple and easy to solve. All he had to do was point the .38 at Hooker and add a last bit of pressure to the trigger.

He didn't do it. With a fully loaded double-action weapon in his hand, not even McGuire could have missed at that point-blank distance. But he didn't do it.

By this time two full seconds had passed since McGuire had started his bumbling draw. As gunslingers reckon time, a dozen lifetimes. A fine, oily mist of sweat appeared as if by magic on Hooker's face. He couldn't look away from the muzzle of the .38 in McGuire's hand; he stared at that single dark eye like a bird charmed by a snake. He no longer even attempted to fire the .45.

"McGuire . . ." Hooker's voice cracked. He swallowed hard, licked his dry lips and tried again. "McGuire, don't kill me."

The crowd turned in fascination to the gun-slinger. Eyes blinked in amazement. Had they actually heard what they thought they had heard? Had they heard Jeremy Hooker begging for his life?

"McGuire," Hooker said again, in not much more than a whisper, "don't kill me. It ain't fair.

I'm unarmed." As if he had suddenly discovered a live coal in his hand, he dropped the .45 and it fell in a fine shower of reddish dust. "I'm not armed. You can't shoot me now, McGuire. It'd be murder."

McGuire stared at the gunslinger in amazement. He was faintly surprised to discover that he had the .38 raised and pointed generally at Hooker's middle. If he pulled the trigger now, it would not be murder. Not legally. Not in Texas. But McGuire was learning some things about himself that he had only suspected before—for one thing, he was not a killer. He was also learning some things about other people that he hadn't even suspected.

He glanced quickly at the wall of faces. They were waiting tensely, expectantly, even eagerly. Waiting for the touch that would send Hooker to his death. Why were they in such a hurry, and why did they suddenly want Hooker dead? Was it so important to them that they witness the death of a gunshark? Were they afraid that there would be nothing else to talk about in days to come?

McGuire found it all difficult to understand.

Between the two possemen he glimpsed Ellie Moncrief. There was that brightness in her eyes that disturbed him. He had the uneasy feeling that she would have pulled the trigger for him, if that had been possible.

And Arnie Stone—what was it that McGuire

saw in Arnie's face? Disappointment that Hooker's weapon had failed him? Only in Rusty Miller's eyes did McGuire see real relief, a kind of thankfulness that he had not been killed. Well, maybe the madstone had been worth the trouble after all.

A little rivulet of sweat gathered near Hooker's ear then suddenly broke and rushed like a small river down the side of his face. He's scared, McGuire thought in fascination. He's scared of me, Willie McGuire!

"Look, McGuire," the gunslinger managed in a cracking voice. "I ain't armed. I'm turnin' and walkin' away. You can't shoot me."

"Hooker," McGuire told him wearily, "I'm sick of lookin' at you, and that's the God's truth." With lordly arrogance, he waved with the revolver. "The quicker you get out of my sight, the better I'll like it."

A certain wildness came over the gunslinger when he fully realized what was happening. The many faces of the crowd turned on him. They were grinning. Some were sneering. One of the Circle-M drovers—it sounded like Shorty Eller— began laughing. Soon the whole crowd was looking at Hooker and laughing.

That, McGuire thought to himself, kills Jeremy Hooker deader than any bullet could have done. Trembling and impotent, the gunslinger heeled on his crutches and hobbled back toward the hotel.

The little hotel owner barred his way on the sidewalk and shouted for all to hear, "I don't want you in my hotel again, Hooker!"

Hooker looked for a moment as if he might literally explode. The crowd, in a sudden rush of relief at learning that it was no longer afraid of him, laughed all the harder. In the end, Hooker lurched away from the hotel and hobbled fiercely toward the livery barn.

Suddenly McGuire found himself the center of a happy storm. Rusty Miller and Shorty Eller, with others of the Circle-M crew, rushed up and pounded him on the back and congratulated him on facing down the gunslinger. Even Arnie Stone seemed mildly relieved that the affair was over. Several townsmen stepped forward and shook his hand enthusiastically. Ellie Moncrief broke away from the two possemen, rushed to McGuire and threw her arms around his neck. "McGuire, you did that for me! Just for me!"

McGuire stared at her dumbfounded. Ellie did not seem to notice. "I'll make it up to you, McGuire! I promise, I'll make it up!"

McGuire was slightly dazed. He had never had a "decent" woman swing on his neck before. He had never experienced the intoxication of popularity, of having important townsmen jostling one another for the privilege of shaking his hand and telling him what a fine fellow he was.

"Thanks to you, McGuire, we got ourselves shed of that gunslinger. He won't be stayin' here after what's happened today."

An officious little rooster-chested man plowed his way through the crowd and seized McGuire's hand and wrung it with passion. "Tar City's in your debt, sir! If there's ever anything we can do . . ."

McGuire learned later that this was the mysteriously invisible county sheriff who hadn't been seen in Tar City since Hooker had started running things there.

All in all it was a memorable few minutes in the life of Willie McGuire. He felt slightly light-headed and foolish—in a pleasant sort of way—much the same as he had felt once before after he had gulped down three bottles of champagne wine, on a bed, in an Ellsworth saloon.

Only Gonzales appeared to be untouched by the excitement of the moment. Standing to one side of the wrecked calaboose, he calmly built a cigarette, licked it into shape and lit it. He smoked the cigarette leisurely, arms folded across his chest. Many times in the past he had seen McGuire in unusual situations. The novelty passed with time and normalcy returned. Or what passed as normalcy in the world of Willie McGuire.

At last the crowd began to thin out. Someone noticed that the sun had quietly set behind the livery barn. A night silence settled on the rude, unpainted cowtown. A tense, desperate situation had been met and dealt with; the day was coming to a close. Townsmen drifted off to their homes or to saloons to relive the episode at their leisure.

McGuire uncharacteristically refused a number of offers of free drinks at the Drover Saloon. Granted, refusing the drinks had not been McGuire's idea at first. Ellie Moncrief, still swinging from one of his arms, looked at him unblinkingly with those wide, bright eyes and said, "They're fair-weather friends, McGuire; you're better off to ignore them. Besides," she added, suddenly returning to her normal briskness, "it's time we got started back to the herd."

Ellie signaled to Arnie Stone. "Have the boys round up the ridin' stock. We're headin' back north while there's still some light to see by."

Grudgingly, the trail boss turned to do her bidding. She regarded his broad retreating shoulders with dissatisfaction. "McGuire," she asked abruptly but quietly, "how'd you like to be trail boss the rest of the way to Dodge?"

McGuire looked startled and possibly even a little outraged at such a suggestion. "No ma'am, thanks all the same. Bossin' drovers ain't the kind of work I was cut out for."

She gazed at him with narrowed eyes. "Think about it. We'll talk about it later." Suddenly she thought of some more chores for Arnie Stone and went off to deliver the orders.

McGuire turned to Gonzales and frowned. "What's the matter with *you?* You look like you just bit into a green persimmon."

Gonzales shrugged. "Thinkin', I guess. It ain't every day I see Willie McGuire get offered a job as trail boss."

"She never meant it the way it sounded." McGuire shifted feet in discomfort. "She just let herself get carried away in the excitement."

"Most likely," his sidekick allowed dryly. "But what do you aim to do if she lets the offer stand?"

"Hell's afire!" McGuire waved his arms listlessly. "Once you get your teeth in somethin', you just won't let go, will you?" Huffily, he started toward the wagon yard. Gonzales fell in beside him.

"That ain't exactly an answer to what I asked you."

"Maybe. But it's all the answer you're goin' to get tonight."

"Then you aim to take the trail bossin' job from Arnie Stone?"

"I never *said* that."

They walked on for several seconds. Eller and the day wrangler had brought up the outfit's saddle horses and the hands were beginning to mount. Ellie Moncrief, already mounted, rose in her stirrups and called, "Shorty's got you a horse saddled, McGuire. You're ridin' up front with me."

Gonzales grinned bleakly. McGuire glowered at him. "Maybe you think I can't *handle* a trail bossin' job."

"I was thinkin' about somethin' else," Gonzales said. "Maybe it hasn't come to you yet, but you made yourself a big reputation today. Facin' down a gunslinger like Jeremy Hooker. It's the same as gunnin' him down, when you look at it in a fair light. A story like that's bound to spread. Before the week's out they'll be tellin' it in every bunkhouse in Texas, how a wagon cook named McGuire faced down the famous Jeremy Hooker."

McGuire blinked. Obviously, this had not occurred to him. "What're you tryin' to say?"

"That every hotshot gunslinger between here and the Platt will be gunnin' for the man that faced down Jeremy Hooker. If it was me, I wouldn't want to put myself at the head of a trail herd."

"Why not?"

"It would be a mighty easy place for gunslingers to find you." Gonzales gazed innocently at the dark sky. "But maybe you ain't goin' to let a little thing like that worry you."

McGuire took a claybank gelding from Shorty Eller and stepped into the stirrup. "Get a move on, McGuire," Ellie Moncrief called. "The outfit's waitin' on you."

"Looks like that's where you'll be from now on," Gonzales said to no one in particular. "Right up front for everybody to see. Alongside of Missus Moncrief."

McGuire snorted. But he quickly swung to the saddle and spurred into the street to where Ellie was waiting. The widow turned and looked back at the long-faced Arnie Stone. "Is everybody mounted?"

"Everybody but Gonzales. He can catch up."

The crew of the Circle-M, headed by Ellie and McGuire, rounded smartly into the street and headed north. Townsmen stood on the sidewalk and watched the departure with obvious relief. All in all, it had worked out much better than they could have hoped. Jeremy Hooker, disgraced, had silently crept out of town under the cover of darkness. The brawling McGuire had let himself be led docilely away by the young widow.

The townsmen smiled. A few of them lifted hands in halfhearted salutes as the column passed up the street. All's well, the relieved expressions seemed to say, that ends well. Tomorrow they would start rebuilding the calaboose and the town would be the same as it had been before the fateful brawl in the Drover Saloon.

Ellie Moncrief and her drovers reached the wagon shortly before midnight. Gonzales, falling naturally into his night-hawking duties, turned the animals back to the remuda. McGuire sat wearily on the wagon tongue and built a cigarette. Ellie Moncrief came up behind him. "Have you thought it over, McGuire? About taking Arnie's place on the crew?"

He sighed. "I thought about it."

"Well?" she asked impatiently.

"I don't know. It ain't an easy notion to get used to."

"There's nothing hard to understand about it. I'm offering you the job of bossin' the crew the rest of the way to Dodge. After that . . ." Her voice trailed off. She looked at McGuire thoughtfully. One of the hands came up to the fire, poured himself some coffee and went away. She went on, "After the drive's over, maybe then I'll make you boss of the outfit, back at headquarters. You'd like that, wouldn't you?"

McGuire closed his eyes for a moment and tried to picture himself in the role. Willie McGuire, manager of the Circle-M. He would be a man of considerable importance. A person to reckon with. "There goes McGuire," they would say enviously, "boss of the outfit."

He lit his cigarette and looked at Ellie. "What about Arnie Stone?"

"Arnie's weak. Or maybe just young and inexperienced. Anyway, the outfit needs a strong man to head it—like my husband was."

Like her husband . . . There was something in

the way she said it that made McGuire uneasy. "I'll have to think on it some more."

"All right," she said reluctantly. "But I'll want to know by tomorrow morning. I don't like to let a thing drag."

Some time later Gonzales came in from the remuda to get some coffee. McGuire was still sitting on the wagon tongue, a cold stub of a cigarette in his mouth. In the distance they could hear the night watch quietly cursing the restless cattle. Everything was back to normal.

Gonzales hunkered down beside the fire and eyed his partner narrowly. "The widow didn't take her offer back, did she?"

"Nope. She's thinkin' about makin' me boss of the whole outfit when we get back to head-quarters."

"*If* we get back, then." McGuire shrugged his shoulders.

"You ain't forgot about the gunslingers that'll come lookin' for you, have you?"

"I ain't forgot, but they don't bother me much. Havin' Hooker gunnin' for me kind of got me used to bein' scared, I guess."

"What is it, then? Somethin's botherin' you."

McGuire sat for a long while saying nothing. After a time Gonzales said, "The widow ain't a hard-lookin' woman. It won't be long before she'll start thinkin' about gettin' married again. Maybe she's already started thinkin' about it."

McGuire grunted.

Gonzales gazed idly at the deep Texas sky. "She's got spirit, you got to give her that. Stands right up to menfolks and tells 'em what for. Look at the way she handles Arnie Stone."

"I ain't Arnie Stone."

Gonzales grinned faintly. "Never said you was." He turned and started back to the remuda when McGuire said, "If I *did* take the job, there'd always be a place for you on the crew."

Gonzales shook his head, his white teeth flashing in the firelight. "I'd sooner find my own jobs. Work when I feel like it." He shrugged. "It wouldn't be the same when the straw boss is your own pard."

McGuire continued to sit, too tired to move. Too tired even to build a fresh cigarette. It had been a long day, a long series of days. He was beginning to think fondly of his bedroll when a corner of the wagon sheet lifted and Ellie Moncrief's head appeared above the sideboards. "McGuire, haven't you started the sourdoughs yet?"

McGuire turned and looked up at her. Her face was softly etched in firelight. A right handsome woman, he thought to himself. That was a fact that few men would dispute.

"McGuire, didn't you hear me?"

"Yes, ma'am," he said. "I guess I was still thinkin' about that job."

"That's all well and good," she told him with

her usual briskness. "But in the meantime the crew's got to eat. They've got a long day ahead of them tomorrow, they'll want a hot breakfast." She raised the canvas flap a little higher and squinted down at him. "Anything the matter, McGuire?"

"No, ma'am," he sighed. "I guess not."

"Then get the sourdoughs set out to rise." She pulled her head into the wagon. The canvas flap came down.

McGuire got groggily to his feet. Sourdoughs! All this time he had been picturing himself as boss of the outfit, and she expected him to make sourdoughs! Grumbling under his breath, he stumbled to the rear of the wagon and groped inside the chuck box for his bread pan. "Boys," he muttered to the world at large, "old Willie McGuire's about had a bait of biscuit-shootin'. Tell you the honest truth, he's had a bait of trail drivin' in general!" He pulled down the bread pan and half-filled it with flour.

That was the way they found it the next morning. The bread pan half-full of flour. "Where's McGuire?" Ellie Moncrief demanded in an outrage. "I told him hours ago to get the biscuits started."

Matchstick, the day wrangler, rode up to the wagon dragging a piece of firewood. "McGuire," he told the widow, "ain't here."

Ellie stared at him. "Where is he?"

253

"That's somethin' I can't say, ma'am. Him and Gonzales lit out. Maybe an hour before first light. Cut their personal horses out of the remuda and headed south. I think there was some talk about Chihuahua."

"Chihuahua?" The word rang like brass on the morning air. "Matchstick, are you loco?"

"No, ma'am, I don't think so. I'm just tellin' you what I seen."

She jutted her chin and stubbornly refused to believe it. After all, she was the owner of the outfit. Circle-M hands didn't just ride off in the middle of the night without a word. Without even bothering to draw their time. "Get the crew together. I want the prairie searched. I want McGuire found."

A puzzled and groggy crew of drovers was sent out into the chill dawn, and they scoured the prairie until almost midday. They did not find McGuire.

They searched gullies and washes and arroyos. No McGuire. Around noontime the weary drovers gathered back at the wagon. Ellie saw by the look of their faces that it would be useless to prolong the search. "All right," she told them in cold anger. "Get the herd up and start it north. If McGuire shows his face here again, you tell him for me that we ain't hirin'."

A few of the drovers nodded. Others gazed uncomfortably at the dazzling sky. "And while you're at it," Ellie continued hotly, "you can tell Willie McGuire that . . ."

But it was all a waste of good breath on a hot day. None of them ever saw McGuire again.

Center Point Large Print
600 Brooks Road / PO Box 1
Thorndike, ME 04986-0001 USA

(207) 568-3717

US & Canada:
1 800 929-9108
www.centerpointlargeprint.com